MELANCHOLY II

OTHER WORKS IN DALKEY ARCHIVE PRESS'S
NORWEGIAN LITERATURE SERIES

JON FOSSE
MELANCHOLY II

TRANSLATED BY
ERIC DICKENS

DALKEY ARCHIVE PRESS
Champaign / London / Dublin

Originally published in Norwegian as *Melancholia II*
by Det Norske Samaglet, Oslo, 1996

Copyright ©1996, 1997 by Jon Fosse and Det Norske Samaglet \
Published by permission of Rowohlt Verlag GmbH, Reinbeck bei Hamburg
Translation copyright ©2013 by Eric Dickens

First Edition, 2014

Library of Congress Cataloging-in-Publication Data

Fosse, Jon, 1959-
  [Melancholia II. English]
  Melancholy II / Jon Fosse ; translated by
Eric Dickens. -- First edition.
    pages cm
  Translated from the Norwegian.
  ISBN 978-1-56478-904-4 (acid-free paper)
  I. Dickens, Eric, translator. II. Title.
  PT8951.16.O73M4613 2013
  839.82'374--dc23
                        2013040497

Partially funded by the Illinois Arts Council, a state agency and the University of Illinois
at Urbana-Champaign \ This translation has been published with the financial support of
NORLA (Norwegian Literature Abroad) Foundation

www.dalkeyarchive.com

Printed on permanent/durable acid-free paper
Cover: design and composition Mikhail Iliatov

MELANCHOLY II

Stavanger, early fall 1902: Oline is walking up the hill from the sea, leaning on her stick she walks upwards step by step, and her feet ache so much that she will hardly manage to get up there, but she does, step by step Oline moves upwards, in one hand she is holding her stick, in the other she has the fish on a string, and oh how it aches, thinks Oline, and oh how steep it is, this hill up from the sea and up to her house, and every day she has to struggle up this hill, where the houses are built on both sides, close to one another, on a steep hill up from the sea, and right up there, at the top, is where Oline herself lives in her little white house. And Oline is struggling her way uphill, step by step. In one hand she is holding her stick, in the other she is carrying the two fish from Svein the fisherman, today she got the fish, not one øre did Svein the fisherman want for the fish, maybe he realized that she is short of money nowadays, but did she say anything about that, no, not a word did Oline say, not a word did she say, Oline is thinking. And just a little bit further now, then I'll take a rest, thinks Oline. But she must hold out for a little longer. And if she just stops, then the aching in her feet will ease. And the longer she stands the more the aching will ease. Just a bit more now, then she'll take a rest, before she walks that last bit, thinks Oline. Svein the fisherman, yes. All that fish she must have bought from him, thinks Oline and then hears someone calling her.

Oline, someone calls.

Oline! someone calls again

and Oline stops. Because goodness someone was calling her.

Oline! someone calls once more.

And Oline looks at the nearby house, and there, in the window on the second floor stands Signe with her head out of the window.

Oline! Signe is calling.

You, Oline, she says.

Wait a bit, Oline, says Signe.

I'll come down to you, says Signe

and Oline sees Signe disappear from the window and Signe, well, thinks Oline, it was Signe who was calling, and just think that she didn't hear it was Signe calling, no, there's not much to her nowadays, she remembers nothing, that's what it's like now, she remembers nothing, thinks more about how it's been, nothing, she can't remember, not from lunch till dinner, as they say, all she can remember is what she did during her childhood, her youth, but on the contrary remembers it as if it has just happened, thinks Oline, but now Signe has called out to her, and what she can remember is that she and Signe have never been the best of friends, thinks Oline, not that they've been enemies either, no they haven't, but for one reason or another they haven't got on particularly well, maybe because Signe has always been so refined, like, Signe has always thought that Oline wasn't diligent enough, that her house wasn't clean enough, that her kids weren't clean enough, not that she's ever said as much, Signe hasn't, but that she's meant it, no there's no doubt about that in her mind, thinks Oline, no, Signe has never thought that there was much to Oline either, no, thinks Oline, and she herself has never really liked Signe much either, and if truth be told, they could actually be counted as enemies, thinks Oline, no, not really enemies, but they have never really been friends, and never before has Signe called out to her when she has more or less every single day been walking with the fish she has bought down by the sea, she has gone past Signe's house endless times, and never before today has Signe called out to her, and hardly has she ever met Signe either, when she has gone all those times down to the sea and then back up again with her fish afterwards, Signe could well have been trying to avoid her, thinks Oline, but Signe has called out to her now, so what's up now? thinks Oline, as she stands there with the fish in one hand and the stick in the other, and Oline is wondering why in all the world has Signe now gone and called out to her? what is it she wants? why should she, suddenly, go and call out to her? thinks

Oline and she sees Signe coming out of the house, and now Oline sees that Signe has grown old, she who was so pretty when she was young, is now old and stooped, thinks Oline, and she sees Signe walking over toward her in an apron. What can it be that Signe wants now? thinks Oline.

Sivert, says Signe

and Oline thinks that she means her brother, but the fact that the brother she was such good friends with when she was little should go and get married to someone like Signe is something she really hasn't quite been able to understand, thinks Oline.

Sivert's poorly, says Signe.

I don't think he'll be with us much longer.

Oline looks at Signe. That Sivert was poorly was not anything new, but that things had got so far with him, no, that was not good news.

Is that what you're saying, says Oline.

Signe nods.

And he's getting sicker and sicker, today he's got a lot sicker, says Signe.

No, that's horrible, says Oline

and she feels a shudder go through her, no Sivert's not going to depart now as well, first Lars did, and now it's Sivert, they were about the same age, first Lars departed, but Sivert has been healthy and vigorous for such a long time, never sick ever, just work and toil all the day long, is he now going to depart?

And I think that the end is nigh for him, says Signe.

And Sivert, says Signe

and she breaks off and Oline thinks that he might want to speak with her, his sister, if he's going to be departing, nothing strange about that, if he's departing he'll want to say farewell to his sister and then she'll just have to go into Signe's house, and she hasn't set foot in that house in as long as she can remember, if she didn't happen to be there yesterday, in which case she wouldn't remember either. Everything that has just happened she forgets, thinks Oline. But that Sivert is going to depart. Well, that can't be going to happen right away. She, Signe, is exaggerating a bit, she's always been one to worry and exaggerate, and she's always put on airs, and now she's got the idea that Sivert's going to depart right away.

He asked if I would ask you to drop in, says Signe.

He's lying in the attic, she says

and Oline nods.

You do want to, don't you? asks Signe.

Of course I'll come, says Oline.

He, Sivert asked me to ask you to come, says Signe.

You can give him my regards, say I'm coming, says Oline.

Signe looks at Oline.

You can do so now, right away, she says.

But I'll have to go home first, tidy myself up a bit, I'll be going home with the fish anyway, says Oline.

Yes, and don't be too long about it, says Signe.

I'll be back presently, says Oline.

Yes, you really must do so, he wants to see you so much, says Signe.

You can give him my regards, say I'm coming, says Oline.

Yes, you must come, says Signe

and Oline sees how Signe turns around and rushes in again into her house and Oline is thinking no, Sivert can't be departing as well, no she should never have imagined that, but he can't be that sick, she's exaggerating a bit, that Signe, anyhow she can no doubt go home first with the fish. And it's pressing a bit down there so she'll have to drop by the privy too and, would she want to go to Signe's privy instead, no, that she doesn't want to do, thinks Oline, no that she doesn't want to, thinks Oline. She has to get home with the fish. Then she can go around to the privy. Then she can maybe change her skirt, because for all I know there could be something in what Signe says, that Sivert is at death's door, and her brother has, after all, asked his wife to ask her to come, otherwise Signe would never have done so, thinks Oline, so she'll just drop in, she'll then go into Signe's house, where she has not set foot in all these years, and she, Oline, must come now that her brother Sivert, her good brother, has asked her to come, she must come, and you used to look up to him during childhood, even though he was younger she used to look up to him, that must have been because he was so big and strong, a stylish lad he was, not to mention that when he grew older and became a young man with those strong arms, and who was famous for being strong, thinks Oline, he really was a man, he, Sivert, thinks Oline, but maybe she should have gone up right away? is he really at death's door? she maybe won't get there on time if she goes home with the fish, she thinks, and it's so painful to walk, her feet really do ache, just a little bit more, thinks Oline, no, she should have gone up to Sivert right away, why didn't she do so? because it was Signe who asked her? because she was so unwilling to be in Signe's house? was that what it was? thinks Oline, and all she can do now is toddle off home with the fish, and it really does feel as if she needs to go, it's pressing down there, both at the back and at the front, if she's not mistaken, thinks Oline, and she mustn't do it in her drawers, it mustn't happen of its own accord, she's got to get home, and go in with the fish, and then go around to the privy, yes, thinks Oline, and it was really good to be able to stand quietly for a bit, if she stops her feet stop aching, thinks Oline. But now she'll have to go uphill a little longer. And even if she has stopped somewhere she has never done before, she can't begrudge herself another stop at the spot she usually stops to rest, thinks Oline, and now she will have to get her body moving, thinks Oline, she cannot stay here any longer, but it's a sad thing about Sivert, is he going to depart now? not long since Lars departed, and now Sivert's going to depart? then it'll be her turn too, thinks Oline. Yes, if only it were her turn, thinks Oline. If only she were departing now, thinks Oline and puts her stick forward, then the one foot, oh how hard it is, it's as if she'll have to break loose that foot, shove it forward, that's what it feels like, push it forward, is what it feels like, as if it wants to tear her to pieces, is what it feels like, and it's almost worse than it's ever been, and it's probably because she has stopped where the hill is at its steepest, if only it had just been that constant ache, but this wrenching, this tearing pain is just too much, thinks Oline and puts her other foot forward and Oline moves uphill, gently, while both feet ache, she moves uphill with her stick in her one hand and the fish in the other, moving upwards, and that Sivert's going to depart? no that's too horrible, thinks Oline, no that Sivert is going to depart, that's not right, couldn't Our Lord let her go instead, she who is in such a hurry, thinks Oline, and she'll just have to walk a bit further, then she'll stop, now she can see her own house, where she will stop and rest, as she usually does, thinks Oline, only a little bit more, well, then the ache will finally ease, thinks Oline, and her feet are aching and Oline thinks it feels as if the whole of her body is aching everywhere it can ache, thinks Oline, and she can probably stop soon, thinks Oline, and now she can soon stop, now that she'll soon be there, but that she will have to walk the same stretch of road twice again today, no, that really is too much, but if Sivert is at death's door, she will have to go and talk with him, he's asked to see her, and she'll have to go to him, thinks Oline. And she can stop now, even though she had an unexpected stop at the steepest part of the hill, she'll not begrudge herself a stop where she usually does, thinks Oline. And Oline stops. And Oline stands there. And Oline feels how the pain in her feet eases. And Oline looks upwards at her house and her house is nice, but small, she lives in a rather small but nice house, thinks Oline, especially since she had her house painted white it became nice, she thinks, and stands there leaning on her stick and having a rest. And Oline feels how the pain in her feet lessens, everything is getting better, but then she thinks that she will have to go up and down the hill today once more, and she must be able to manage that, thinks Oline, just a little break, now, must rest a bit, because her feet ache, as soon as she walks a little, the ache in her feet starts up, and she is out of breath, that too, and it is steep up the hill from the sea up to her house, earlier she used to walk up the hill from the sea without even noticing it and it was something she did all the time, but now. And it's getting worse and worse, day by day. No, that it should have come to this with her, thinks Oline. And Sivert is going to be departing too. No sooner is Lars laid in the earth, but Sivert follows suit.

Yes, yes, says Oline.

And now she must rest for a bit, now, at the spot she usually rests, because she will be going up the last steep stretch to her house, before she walks up the last and steepest bend, outside the house of Bård the fisherman, where she usually stops. It's here she stops, not any further down, where she stopped today, but the fact that she stopped down there was because Signe had called out to her, not because she wanted to stop, thinks Oline. And did Signe say that he, Sivert, wanted to talk to her? That Sivert was at death's door? And she did say she'd come, didn't she? That she'd just pop home first with the fish? But now she has stopped. And it's nice to stand quietly, feel the ache in her feet ease. When she walks upwards from the sea, she always looks forward to that, a little bit more, well, then you can take a rest, is what she tends to say to herself, just a bit more, she thinks when her feet ache worst, so Oline forces herself to walk uphill, because she'll soon have a rest, and outside Bård the fisherman's house is where she usually stops. And Oline stops, just like on other days, and she stands leaning on her stick. She stands there and leans on her stick, and she notices how the ache in her feet eases and her breathing grows calmer. Oline is supporting one hand on her stick, and is holding the string with the fish in the other. And Oline looks upwards to her house, it's quite a small house that she has, she is thinking, but that's how it ended up with her, she ended up living in one of the smallest houses in the whole of Stavanger town, that she knows, but maybe there are even smaller houses in Stavanger town? there surely must be, because she's not been walking so far and wide these past few years, not after her feet had begun to get so bad, after that she has not walked any further than strictly necessary, nor did she walk very far earlier either, hadn't had the chance of doing so, with all those kids she, Oline, has had, because she, Oline, has given birth to a lot of kids in that little house of hers, cramped though it has been, small inside in every way it can be, but big too! no denying that! really been big! really has! thinks Oline, and that strange brother of hers who could have become a great painter; and sure, he's painted the most beautiful of paintings, but in the end they became daubs, in the privy, right above the door, by the way, she has a daub of a painting hanging, some figures, a horse with a horseman it must be, painted on the back of the label from a tobacco box, no, not much to look at, this daub, but it's been hanging there for so long that it can carry on doing so, but how often hasn't she thought of taking it down! goodness me!

that someone who had painted so many beautiful pictures should end up doing such daubs! no, that was sad, but that's how it went, and when you have the opportunity you don't deny it, that's how it is, that's how it is, thinks Oline, and now she is breathing quite calmly, and now she must get home with the fish she went down to the sea to get, and she got cheap fish today too, the cheapest fish, and she managed not to pay for the fish today, he's a good guy, Svein the fisherman, she's always managed to buy cheap fish from Svein the fisherman, oh yes. That brother of hers. The only thing she has got left from him is that daub hanging on the door in her privy. One day when he was short of tobacco he came and asked her if she needed anything doing, some sawing or similar, but at the time she had enough firewood, he should have come right now! earlier Lars would have been able to saw and chop as much as he could manage! but that day she hadn't got any work for him, and so she gave him a little tobacco, and then he gave her the picture that's now hanging in the privy, and it wasn't a pretty picture either, but she would have to hang it somewhere or other, so she had hung it out in the privy, thinks Oline. He, Lars, was a strange man. Crazy, they said. Crazy, yes indeed. Crazy Lars was what they called him. And then that unmentionable name. Rat Lars. Rat. Rat in your pocket. Rat. And that she has grown as old as she has, her mother never grew that old, but he, Crazy Lars, did grow old. And Father. It must come from Father's side of the family. Must have done. Must do, thinks Oline and she straightens her back, she looks at that little house of hers, a small and beautiful house, she thinks, after it was painted white it became so pretty, she thinks, and begins to take short steps up the hill. No, now she really has become old, her feet ache so, but walk she must, she has to buy food to keep herself alive, she has to get firewood to keep the stove going, no, what would happen otherwise? she daren't think of it, if she can't look after herself it would mean sheer poverty, she'll just have to manage, nothing else for it, thinks Oline and she pushes her body onwards up the hill and looks at her house and it's a beautiful house, she is thinking, after it was painted white it became a beautiful house, little, with a small window and in the window there are tulle drapes, yes, drapes made of tulle! in the window! And there are flowers on the windowsill! Earlier on she would have been able to say what the flowers were. Pansies? Can that be what some of them were called? Begonias? Daisies? No, no, thinks Oline, but for sure she lives in a beautiful house, thinks Oline, and she leans on her stick and walks up the hill toward the house where she lives, with two fish on a string Oline is walking upwards, and the going is tough, and step by step by step she is getting there and the two small fish are dangling from side to side on the string. If only she hadn't got that ache in her legs. When she sits they don't ache so terribly, but when she is walking, they ache endlessly. And she's so out of breath, and her memory, she can't remember very much at all, not only has she forgotten the names of the flowers on the windowsill, no, everything's vanished goodness knows where, but then it pops up, without reason, memories from long ago, from her childhood, from her youth, they keep on popping up, and often she remembers something that happened goodness knows how long ago better than something that happened yesterday, what did happen yesterday? no, can she say what happened? did anything happen yesterday? yes, yesterday she no doubt went to buy fish? milk? did she boil the fish? she must have done, and she was sitting there with her knitting, her crocheting, she was doing her knitting and maybe someone dropped by? one of her sons? daughters? a grandchild? a sister? a brother? but she hasn't got brothers any longer! how can she think like that! all her brothers are surely dead? yes, they must be dead, every single one of them, it isn't more than a couple of years ago that her last brother died, the one who lived somewhere out Haugesund way, was it, why can't she remember, she can't remember anything at all, soon she won't even be able to remember where she herself lives, thinks Oline, but yes, she can remember that, because she lives in her little white house, in one of the smallest houses in Stavanger, and she lives alone, but earlier she used to live with her husband and children, and it got crowded when they were all at home, but it was lively, yes it was, thinks Oline. Lively in that little house of hers, yes it was. You can't deny that. Lively in her house, that's right, thinks Oline and she stops and she's right in front of her house, is looking at the red-painted door, a red door leads into her little house, thinks Oline, because at the same time as the house was painted white, the door was painted red. And now she's going to open the door, and go inside. But maybe she should pop around to the privy first? they've all had an inside toilet installed, as they say, many people have, the first time she'd heard of such a thing, an indoor toilet, a water closet, was when Lars had come home from the Austpå hospital, there they had a toilet with water in it, he said, you sat down on white glaze and did your business, and afterwards water came gushing and washed away what you had done, he told, but now several other people have had such a water closet, maybe not so many, that's true, but at least some people have got a water closet, but no indoor water closet for her, no, no indoor water closet for Oline, no, it's not got that far, not her, no, she's managed so long with the privy, and will make do with it for the rest of her days, and with a pot, now ugh! glad no one can hear what I'm thinking, but a pot has its uses, all those times at night, if it hadn't have been so difficult to sit properly on the pot, they should have seen her putting the pot on the table in the room and sitting neatly down on it! with her one hand on her stick, the other on the edge of the table, they should have seen her! but now it's happening in the daytime and she resorts to the pot, and, and the pot doesn't get emptied right away, far from it, but everything's getting less, yes, it does smell. No, first get the fish in the house, then sit down and rest it out a bit. Then pop out to the privy. But is it pressing down there? And she's going to pop out to the privy, and sure, she used to take the fish in first, but she can't just take the fish with her into the privy, and just think if someone saw her taking the fish to the privy! that too has happened! that poor little wretch! are you going to the privy with your fish again! that's what he said! to an old woman who had given birth to so many children! a little wretch! the neighbors' boy! taking the fish into the shithouse with you, he said, but she is so keen to go, she can take the fish in the privy with her, hang them on the hook on the door, as she has done so often, because she has often hung the fish on the door hook, nothing wrong with that, when she thinks that she has made a habit of going down to the sea for her fish and goes off to the privy when she gets home and hangs up the fish on the door hook inside the privy, but like doing so, no, she doesn't, thinks Oline and leans on her stick and looks at the red-painted door of her house. And Oline looks at the corner of the house, it's just around the corner, and so, just around the corner of the house, just near a hilltop, there stands her privy. The privy was built with driftwood once upon a time. She can't remember when it was built, but it was driftwood they used. But the privy is still standing. And it's not going to fall down just yet, not just yet. Just imagine sitting above water as you are about to do your business, they could get her to do lots of things but sitting above water? in what they call a water closet? no, never. Not Oline. She remembers how shocked she was when Lars told her that at the Austpå hospital he had done his business in a water closet. No water closet for her, no. Not for Oline, no, thinks Oline and she hears scurrying feet approaching, and she thinks it may be one of her grandchildren running up to her? she has so many grandchildren and they live all around the neighborhood, many of them, and she has so many grandchildren, and she has lost count, and sad to tell the names of her grandchildren are, shameful to tell, also getting a bit muddled, the names come and go, yes, she has to admit that, but she doesn't forget their faces, every single one of them, her grandchildren, and she remembers faces! every feature! every feature she can remember, and it can happen that one of her grandchildren comes with meat for her from a pig, a sheep, well, that must have happened! and it'll happen again! She believes it will, thinks Oline and she sees a little boy coming running around the corner of the house facing the road where it bends, because the house is on a bend, and yes, she, Oline can see the boy coming running past her down the road at a horrible pace, and she doesn't recognize him, and she looks at the back of the boy as he runs down the road and there are so many young kids in Stavanger town, so many kids, they're all having kids, they all look the same, they have kids in great flocks, flocks of kids, yes, as many as Our Lord allows. She, Oline, watches the boy running down the road. And Oline sees the boy stop and sees him turn his head and look at her.

You can run, you can, shouts Oline.

And the little boy nods.

Horrible the way you're running, she shouts.

The boy nods again.

Horrible, she shouts

and the boy turns again and Oline can see him make a jump and start to run down the road and he turns his head in her direction as he is running down the road and then he shouts Oline with the fish! does the boy and begins to sing, Oline with the fish in the privy, and didn't she know that already, wasn't that the poor little boy, she is thinking and she, Oline with the fish, hears the boy singing, she Oline with the fish in the privy, he is singing, but didn't the lad look like that, the one who had once before called out to her? because wasn't that kid much older and not like a little puppy, the one who spoke so coarsely to her earlier on was much bigger, not like a little puppy, Oline is thinking, and she hears the boy singing, Oline in the privy, and if it hadn't have been pressing down there, and if she had been sure that nothing would be coming, she would definitely have gone into the kitchen with the fish, but she's got to do something, and once she's got inside it's quite a job to get out again, it's cold, but how cheeky the kids are nowadays, thinks Oline and she can hear the boy singing, Oline with the fish in the privy and she sees that the boy stops and has turned toward her.

Are you going to take that fish into the privy with you? he cries.

You watch out or I'll take you in there too, cries Oline.

Take me then, cries the boy

and Oline sees him leap toward her, before he turns and she sees the boy disappear down the road and she sees him swing around the corner of the Stone House and is gone, and those kids nowadays have become so terribly cheeky, no respect for their elders, thinks Oline and she goes to the corner of the house and she rounds the corner of the house and she goes straight toward the privy and sure, her feet are aching as usual, she thinks and she lifts the hook and she enters the privy and puts her stick aside in the corner near the door and she closes the door and she puts it on the hook and now at last she is alone! at last no one can see what she is doing! at last! Thinks Oline and she hangs the fish on the door hook and she feels it pressing and she pulls up both her skirts and she pulls down her drawers and no oh no because she sees it's a bit wet down there.

No, oh no, no, says Oline.

No oh no, ugh, she says.

Yes, yes, says Oline

and she sits herself over the hole. And Oline feels with her whole body how good it is to be able to sit down, as soon as she has sat down the aching eases a bit.

Yes, yes, says Oline

Life can still be good, she says.

And all she must do now is sit and wait, soon something is going to happen, thinks Oline, and she looks at the two small fish that are hanging on a string over there on the door hook. Those big fish eyes. The blood running down the fish.

Yes, if it hadn't been for the fish, says Oline.

No, then wouldn't it have been easy, she says.

If it hadn't been for the fish.

We'd have had a hard time of it without the fish, says Oline

and she wonders how they would have got enough food for the kids if God hadn't blessed them with fish and she has got to do something but nothing is coming, even if she tries, neither wet nor dry wants to come, thinks Oline, maybe it would have come out more easily if she hadn't brought the fish into the privy, you should do that, just think, taking the fish along, her food, into the privy! but a little has ended up in her drawers nevertheless! well maybe there's nothing more to come, and she didn't even notice when it came? sure, something has often ended up in her drawers before, but then she had always noticed when it came, felt the warmth, ugh! down there, that's how it is, but now? didn't she notice at all that something was coming? thinks Oline.

No, ugh, she says.

And it must have been the ache in her legs that made her fail to notice that something came out, thinks Oline. And it feels as if there is more to come. But nothing's coming. And the fish.

She hasn't got the appetite to eat up this fish. She can't carry on like this, taking food with her into the privy. But she's got to eat something. Every day she's got to go and get some fish to keep her alive. She can't just stop eating. No, that just isn't possible. But that it could get so far with her that she wouldn't enter the kitchen with the fish after she'd been down to the sea to fetch fish and go to the privy only when she got home, and that she wouldn't go to the privy when she was in the house but instead felt she had to go and put a pot up on the table in the room, no, she could never imagine doing that, she could never imagine it would be like that, that it would cost her so much effort to go that little way out to the privy she couldn't have thought that, thinks Oline, but who thinks about such things when you are young, she didn't, at least, she thinks, but if only something would come now, so that she didn't take those fish into the privy to no purpose. No, now something has to come out, thinks Oline. The fact that her feet ache so will just have to be as it is, even if her feet ache she can manage to toddle along, but that it would have to come when it itself wants to and not when she wants it to, that really is almost too crazy, no, that it would end like this no one could have imagined, no. And now something will have to come out soon. And those fish eyes. The big fish eyes. And that blood.

No and twice no, says Oline.

No, I suppose, she says.

But she will just have to sit there a little longer, something could come out, thinks Oline. She will have to stay seated. And it was like that with Lars towards the end, he held back neither his water nor the other thing either, and that he was put with the others up there on the poor loft, at that woman's house near her, what was she called, now, Miriam? Eline, was that her name? a dreadful woman whatever her name was, and Lars was lying in bed there and a little bit came out of his underpants, no, you couldn't expect anything else, but that the kids won't leave her alone, and they didn't leave him, Lars, alone either, after what had been said, no, the kids were after him. Rat in your pocket, that's what they would say. Rat Lars. Rat in your pocket. And those fish eyes. And nothing wants to come out. Yes, Lars, you Lars. Yes you were something special, you were, Lars. And you Lars, you would walk all alone, go and saw wood, all the good firewood you've got your sister, yes, driftwood you collected in summertime, dried it by the shore, and brought it home, sawed it up and stacked it in neat piles. And if you got a bit of food for your work, you'd be satisfied. And if you got a little tobacco, not to mention that. That's what you were like. And when you were a little boy, yes, when you were a little boy on the island, on our island, then I was your big sister and you were my little brother and you had the habit of hiding and staying away for hours on end, until darkness had fallen, and what were you doing, yes, I really spied on you once, I can remember, so clearly, so definitely, as if it were happening today, that one day I decided to follow you, that I can remember, so clearly, so definitely, but what happened yesterday I can't remember, what happened just a little while ago I find hard to remember, if a boy shouted Oline with the fish in the privy, just think a boy came and shouted that to me, and I can often be unsure whether it happened or not, while I can remember so very clearly how I followed my brother one day on the island where we were living, yes, it was called Borgøya, that I can remember, Borgøya or was it Hattøya? in Tysvær anyway, yes, I can remember what it was I saw, can remember what happened, what Lars said is something I can remember, but I'm not all that sure about the name of the island, I would like to think it was Borgøya, but I'm not sure and why am I starting now, sitting here in my privy, without anything happening, why am I beginning to think about Lars, that day I spied on what he was doing, when I decided to follow him on his walk around the island, and did so too, why am I beginning to remember all that now? those big fish eyes? It must be those big fish eyes that are making me remember it. And why are my eyes growing wet now? Why are the tears welling up in my eyes, old crone that I am, as if I were the most delicate of young girls and can't get anything to come out of my aching body, neither wet nor dry. But the ache in my feet has eased. And it's good for an old body to sit down. And Lars that day, the day I followed him there on Borgøya, that was what the island was called no doubt, I followed Lars, and a little is running out, as if it has come all by itself, without me wanting to and it's coming running of its own accord, then no more, and so, a little one! well hasn't an ever so small turd come rolling out! no, who would have believed it! a little one, round as a fish eye! ha! and Lars's eyes, yes, his eyes, the brown eyes that stare and stare and then he began to cry, and he was in a hurry, just like that, he could begin to cry, in the middle of a meal, any time at all he could begin to cry and no one understood what it meant, suddenly the tears would well up in Lars's eyes. No, he was a strange brother. And that day I followed him. I kept out of sight. He didn't notice me. And if he had I would have got it in the neck, because Lars couldn't half get stubborn and bad tempered. He wasn't easy, no not an easy one. He got so angry that he would threaten with anything. Then you had to watch out for him. And if he had become a murderer, that wouldn't have surprised me either. And stubborn, that he really was. Always a bit special, Lars was. Yes, that has to be said. But that day I followed him his brown eyes were black, when I had seen him that morning there was a great darkness in his eyes, dark as a black stone, dark as the blackest of skies were his eyes, and around his eyes was movement as if something were pressing from behind them, as if he were about to start crying, such were his eyes when he stood before me that morning.

Aren't you happy? I asked.

And I saw Lars look down hastily as he stood there and didn't answer.

Why are you like that? I asked him

and I saw Lars shrug his shoulders as he stood looking down at the floor.

You look so sad, I said.

Yes, yes, he said.

Anything in particular? I asked.

No, he said.

Nothing, I suppose, he said.

But, I said

and I saw Lars look up at me with great darkness in his eyes, with the weight of black mountains and from a black sky in his eyes, yes like, as I was thinking, so I saw Lars look up toward me and saw that his eyes had become wet and saw Lars standing there and looking down and I heard Father saying to Mother in the room that they'll soon come and fetch the cattle, that's what they do to folk that think for themselves and don't have their kids christened, that's what happens, you should have your kids christened, but in the church you should only have two small chairs right at the back, they mean that he who gives life its light shall have it, they don't understand anymore I can hear Father saying and I can see how Lars's mouth stretches into a little grin, and goodness Lars is standing there now grinning through his tears and looking at me. I nod to Lars.

What is it, Lars, I say.

Nothing, he says.

Yes, there's something up, I say.

No, says Lars.

It's nothing, he says.

Why should there always be something up? he says.

Shouldn't there be? I say

and I see that Lars is shaking his head.

It's nothing, he says.

But why is everything so wrong? I say.

Not because of anything, at least, he says.

Something else, then? I say.

Because there isn't anything up, maybe, he says.

Must it all be so difficult, I say

and I see Lars nodding.

And the black mountain, I say.

Yes, yes, he says.

And the sea when it's black, I say.

Yes then, he says.

Is that the reason? I say.

Maybe, he says.

Is someone getting at you? I say.

I've nothing against someone getting at me, he says

and I hear Lars say that he has nothing against someone getting at him and I suppose I understand what he means and Lars looks at me with those fish eyes of his and I see his face become

tauter and he doesn't want that to happen, he stares at me, and I
see his face become taut and the tears welling up in his eyes and
see Lars turning away and running towards the door and he opens
the door and I see Lars run out, and I go out and see Lars running
across the marsh, down toward the beach, and he doesn't take the
path and jumps over the marsh and he sinks down again and pulls
up his foot and the other foot sinks into the marsh and I see Lars
running into the distance and see him abruptly sit down on a
hummock right in the middle of the marsh and I can see his back
and I can see him putting his hands up to his eyes and see him
drying his tears, I am thinking, but why does Lars start crying
like that? quite without reason, without cause, he often starts to
cry, I think and I can see Lars with his back bent forward holding
his head in his hands, he is covering his eyes with his hands and I
see Lars turn around and look at me and I hear him, Lars, calling
out that I must leave him in peace! is what Lars is shouting, he is
never left in peace, and there's nothing wrong with him, nothing
the matter, nothing to prate about! yells Lars and I see him getting up and leap down from the hummock and both his feet sink
in the marsh and he gets loose and I see Lars go down toward the
beach and again his foot sinks in the marsh and again he pulls
it out and staggers down over the marsh and I see that the sea is
calm and I see Lars climb up the scree and sit down on a rock and
I see him looking up at the heavens and at the sea and I see him
screw up his eyes and peer out toward the sea, and am thinking
that I just can't fathom my brother, and I turn and look at our little house standing beneath a hillock, between all those marshes,
that's where our little house is standing. I notice a gust of wind
blow my skirt. I look at our house and through the open door I
can hear voices and can hear Father saying in a loud voice that
we can't go on living here any longer, we are the poorest of the
poor, we'll have to try something else, all that there is here is wind
and hillocks and if it hadn't been for the fish we'd have starved to
death ages ago, is what I can hear Father saying and Mother saying that if there is no choice, we'll just have to move, and I can
hear Father saying that we can pull down the house and take it,
move it, there must be money to be earned in Stavanger says Fa-

ther and I hear Mother saying that if he means what he says then we will have to do that then, says Mother, and I can see Lars sitting on a rock on the scree and looking at the sea and the sea is blue and choppy with a little bit of white in all that blue and the sky is also blue, but there are the lightest of clouds in the sky and it's a fine day, and everything is resting yet moving and I can hear Father saying that we must move away, we have no other choice, we just have to move out, is what I hear Father saying, we can't remain here, says Father, we'll starve to death here, there are many mouths to feed, he says, so something has to be done, we'll just have to pull down our house, and we'll have to flit, to move away, is what I hear my father saying and Mother says that he no doubt knows best, she doesn't know, she says, and Father says he doesn't know what's best, but something has to be done, that he knows, says Father, and in Stavanger town there are plenty of freethinkers, the Quakers are powerful there, all you have to do is stick to your plans and you'll get what you need, I hear Father saying and I see Lars is sitting there on a stone in the scree looking toward the sea, and I would have gladly gone over to him, sat next to him, but Lars would not have liked it if I had done so, when he's like he is now it's better to leave him in peace, I've tried so many times in the past to talk to Lars when he was like this, but he has always answered curtly that he wanted to be left in peace, do I not understand anything, that I'm just a dumb woman, that's what Lars would say, well I know I am but where does Lars go off to on days like this? why does he get like this? what is it that happens to him, when he's like this? why does he just disappear, where does he go? what does he do? why does he stay away for so long? because when Lars is like this, he can often be away for hours, sure often he's like this in the morning and he goes out and stays away until after dark, whether there is work to be done or not, he stays away, and sure Father has often told him not to go hiding away like that, no point, Father has said, and Father has even been somewhat angry, but Father isn't one of those that often gets angry, he's nearly always calm, he doesn't say very much either, just a little, but has said to Lars on several occasions, and I've heard it, that Lars mustn't go hiding himself away like that if they've agreed to do some job or other together, then they have to do it, is what Father has said, whether to bait the fishing lines or pull the nets, that's what Father has said to Lars, and Lars simply says yes, he won't hide away, he won't do it again, is what Lars has said, and Lars simply carried on hiding, as if what Father said was no longer valid, or as if he didn't remember what he and Father had agreed, that's what he's like, Lars, and when I've asked him why he goes and hides away like that, even though he has promised Father not to do so, all he has said is that he can't help it, he just has to get away, is what Lars has said, better to be gone, is what he has said, and he's said it to Father too, because I have heard it with my own ears, and I remember Father saying that if it feels so heavy, he'll just have to go away and hide, but if he and Lars had agreed to do some job beforehand, it would be a little stupid of him, said Father, if he, Lars, disappeared, because he could do with a helping hand with quite a lot of jobs, it's much easier to pick the net if there are two of you than if there's only one, said Father, and Lars said he'd have been glad to be with him, but that there was something pressing behind his eyes, said Lars, he was going to explode, he said, so if Father wanted him to explode, all he would have to do is stop him from wandering around on the island, because that was what he was doing, said Lars, he wandered around the island, that's what he did, and Father said he would have to do the best he could and asked if Lars could come and help row the boat while he pulled up the net that was located quite far out to sea this time, said Father, and Lars said he would do so, and then Father went down the path to the beach and I remember how Lars remained standing there looking down as if he were ashamed of himself, as if he felt the pain of what he was doing, and you could see from his face that it hurt Lars.

I've got to help Father, said Lars.

I nodded to him.

But you mustn't just go and disappear, I said.

No, said Lars.

No, I mustn't just go and disappear, he said.

I mustn't, he said.

No, you must help Father, I said.

Yes, said Lars

and I saw Lars turn around and I saw him beginning to climb the hillock behind our house and I thought how just now Lars had said that he would have to help Father and then began to cry as he was saying this and started to run away after all, and now he will be away for a long time, and he won't come back until after it is dark, and Father will have to pull in the net on his own far out to sea and it had happened many times that Lars had stayed away for the whole night and come back exhausted and in a terrible state in the morning and he would be frozen and bleeding, and it had happened that Lars came home bleeding, and both his eyes were dark and wild, and when I asked him where he had been he said not a word, simply looked at me with those dark eyes, and whenever I said it again he said nothing back, nor did he ever answer when Father asked him, and he didn't answer when Mother asked him either, and it happened once that Father didn't give up asking him, he asked again and again and again where he, Lars, had been, what have you been doing Lars? and Lars began to cry and ran out again and I don't remember what time he came home and now I can see Lars sitting on a rock in the scree and if he can see me standing looking at him he will run away, so he mustn't see me looking at him, but I am so curious to find out what Lars does when he runs away the whole day, so I'll just have to run after him and I am standing watching Lars and I had better stop doing so I can't really go and follow him can I? I am thinking and I can see Lars sitting on the rock in the scree and he is looking out to sea and I think that soon Lars will get to his feet and climb off the scree and will simply run down to the beach and something might well happen, Oline is thinking as she sits waiting for something else to come out, but nothing more is coming out, she thinks, it only does so in her drawers, thinks Oline, and that it should all end like this, she thinks, once she was so young that she could run as long as she wanted to, over the hummocks, between the junipers there on Borgøya island, she could squeeze through the densest thicket, all over Borgøya she would be, however impassable the place was, and could keep on as long as she wanted to, could simply keep on going, thinks Oline, and now she is sitting here in the privy, staring at the staring fish eyes, the blood on the fish, it has almost clotted, the blood, and Oline raises her hand and touches one of the fish and she can feel that it has become a little dry and sticky and can see that the fish eyes are no longer staring so intensely, a little dull they have become, the fish eyes, it is as if they are shrinking, she can see, and how long can she have been sitting here? she went down to the sea promptly today as usual to get herself some fish, and went home again and had got as far as her own house, she went to the privy because she could feel it pressing and she took the fish in with her because she didn't want to walk more than she had to, so she didn't drop them off in the kitchen first, because when she walks it does ache so, but no it's not aching anymore, now she has rested out and has got rid of the ache in her feet, thinks Oline and she takes her hand off the fish and rests it on one of her thighs, how wrinkled her thigh has become, it's no longer taut, it bulges, it is streaky, white all over, and Oline notices that she feels nothing when she takes hold of her thigh, and she squeezes them together but still feels nothing, no, no, maybe she's lost all feeling in her thighs too, she thinks as she puts her hand on her other thigh and squeezes and feels nothing and she thinks it must be because of the cold the fact she can't feel anything, well, she'll just have to get up soon, take her fish and go into her house, then she can go into the kitchen and gut the fish, chop it up into pieces, make it ready to boil, and then she can sit down and do a bit of knitting, or maybe she should take out her crocheting? maybe everything has got very cold outside and she can light the stove? it's been for quite a while now that the stove could be lit, but she hasn't got masses of firewood, so she has waited a bit with lighting the stove and simply put on a few more layers of clothing, she does after all have a good knitted cardigan, she knitted it as recently as last year, the old one was so worn and was beyond repair and therefore she, Oline, thought she would not begrudge herself a new cardigan and so she sat and knitted one for herself not to sell to anyone, and that's how it was, but now maybe the time has come to start to fire the stove, thinks Oline and looks at the fish that are hanging there on the door hook and it looks as if the fish are beginning to lose their freshness, thinks Oline, the fish eyes have become so dull, she can see now, and Oline can see Lars sitting on his rock in the scree and he turns around to look at me and he looks at me with his shiny dark eyes and then he, Lars, shouts, why are you watching me, is what he shouts.

No, I'm not doing so, I say.

Yes you are, he says.

No.

Yes, I can see you sitting watching me, says Lars.

Can't I do so, I say.

No, says Lars

and I see Lars bending down and picking up a small stone and he sits there and looks at me with the stone in his hand and he gets up and I can see him raising his hand behind his head and he stares at me and he, Lars, yells that I mustn't sit there staring at him, that's what he yells and Lars throws the stone at me and I duck and I see the stone flying through the air and I see the stone sailing towards our house and I hear the stone smash against the wall and I can see Lars clambering down quickly from his rock in the scree and I can hear Father shouting what's that and I look toward our house and I see Father coming out of our house.

What was that? says Father

and he stands looking at me.

I heard a bang, he says

and I can see in Father's eyes that he is afraid. I nod.

Do you know what that was? he says

and I do know what it was, but I can hardly say that it was Lars who had just thrown a stone at me and had hit the house with it instead, could I?

You don't know? says Father.

I heard a bang, I say.

Yes, quite.

But you don't know what it was?

I shake my head.

It sounded as if a stone or something hit our house, says Father.

I nod.

Yes, I say.

But you didn't see anything? says Father.

I shake my head.

No, this is going too far, says Father.

I nod.

The neighbors are going too far, he says.

The neighbors? I say.

Who else could it have been? says Father.

I look down.

Who else could have thrown a stone at our house, says Father and he shakes his head and goes back inside our house again and I can no longer see Lars, he must have run away down to the beach, and there was me thinking I should follow him, I'll maybe never find him again now, I am thinking, if I stand any chance of finding him at all I will have to go now, I think, see if I can see him anywhere, I will have to do that, I think, and I can hear Father inside our house saying well, well, have the neighbors started throwing stones at our house, has it come to this, says Father and Mother says yes, it really did sound as if someone had thrown a stone or something else at the wall of the house, it was that sort of bang, says Mother, and Father says that Oline was outside, but she didn't see anything, so the stone must have been thrown from the hillock, behind the house, says Father, and I can hear Mother saying that to her it sounded as if the stone had been thrown at the front of the house and he thought so too but as Oline didn't see anything it can't have happened, says Father and Mother says no I suppose nothing has happened and I stand up and look at the sky where the clouds are drifting in their white blue across the sky and I look at the sea with its darker blue and the sea is full of white movements and I think to myself that Lars is like the sea and the sky, forever on the move, from darkness to light, from white to the blackest of black, that's what Lars is like, just like the sea, I think, while I myself am more like a rock or a marsh, not all that uneven, not so even either, but brown and yellow, and I too have my flowers, I think, and I begin to go down the path and I cannot find Lars, and I go down the path and around the scree, along the beach, and I can walk around the outside of the scree, and I look to see if Lars is anywhere on the beach but I can see footprints in the sand, so Lars must have run down the beach, I think, there are fresh footprints in the sand, and I begin to go along the beach and I think what's wrong with Lars? why does he get so angry that he has to throw stones at me? and I too have a temper, even with Father, but could I do any differently? whatever would Father have thought if he got to know that it was Lars who had thrown the stone? I think and hear the breakers rushing onto the beach quite carefully, the sea is quite probably calm, not so rough, no, quite calm and I walk calmly along the beach and now Lars mustn't see me, for then he'd get angry, then he'll start throwing more stones at me, then he will start saying to me that I'm following him, leave me in peace, he will say and I had better not just walk along the beach, then I'll never find Lars, I think to myself, and I leave the beach, and go in among the trees and I go down to the edge of the water and the rocks because I think that Lars is staying near the water, I'm pretty sure he's doing so, even though I don't understand what he does with himself when he's away hour after hour, I nevertheless think he is close to the seashore sitting on the smooth rocks, pushing his way between the bushes, he probably walks round the island, I think to myself, and walk up between the rocks and I am now standing on a rise and can see a pretty steep but smooth rock and from the rock I can see seagulls rise from the rocks and glide up and the seagulls whizz out over the sea and I walk down onto the rocks and below the rocks and there is a little bay, and a little sandy beach along it, and there, there my brother Lars is sitting on a round boulder.

Lars, I cry.

And Lars turns around and looks at me.

Is that you, he says, smiling.

Yes, I say

and I can't understand that Lars isn't angry.

Come on, I'll show you something, says Lars

and he beckons me over and looks at me and I begin to cautiously slide down the rocks, they are steep, but the rocks are dry and I am pressing my hands against them and pressing my feet into uneven patches on the rocks and come down gliding and then I have soft sand under one foot then under the other foot and I look at Lars and he has got up and stands there smiling at me.

Now you're going to see something, says Lars

and he looks at me. I go over to him.

Come, says Lars

and goes up to a slab of rock in the bay. Lars goes in under the slab. Lars turns and looks at me.

Come, says Lars

and Lars beckons me. I go up to Lars and I go and stand next to him under the slab.

Here, says Lars.

Look here, he says

and Lars points at a hole in the rock face and it's all black in there. I can't make anything out.

What is it? I say.

That's charcoal, mixed with a little water, he says.

What's that? I say.

That's what I use, he says.

For what? I say.

I'll show you, says Lars

and gets down on all fours and creeps further under the slab and I can see that it's dark in there and I can hardly make out Lars anymore and then I see him come creeping out from under the slab and understand that he has brought something with him out from under the slab and see that Lars has brought a few piec-es of driftwood out from under the slab and is turning his head and smiling and says that now he is going to show me something, he says.

Now you're going to see something, says Lars.

And he stands up and holds the pieces of driftwood out carefully in front of him and looks at them.

Come, he says

and he looks at me. I go over to Lars and see him smiling as he is looking at the driftwood. I look at the driftwood. I see that there are pictures on the driftwood that he, Lars, is holding out in front of him and smiling at.

Good? says Lars

and he looks at me smiling. I nod. I can see that the pictures he has made on the driftwood are rather good.

Pretty good, I say.

Yes, says Lars.

What does it represent? I say.

Clouds, says Lars.

Pictures of clouds?

Yes.

But they're black?

I did show you that mixture of charcoal and water, says Lars.

I nod.

I use charcoal and water which I stroke with sticks I have frayed the ends of, and I use my fingertips to smear more black on top, says Lars.

I don't think I would have guessed they were clouds, I say.

That doesn't matter much, says Lars.

No, I say.

But if you look closely, says Lars

and he hands me one of the pieces of driftwood and I look closely and yes, when I look closely there are clouds that Lars has made pictures of, clouds with lots of movement in them, as I can see, and they are pretty fine clouds he's made pictures of, and Lars says he's made many such pictures, mostly of clouds, but also of mountains and boats, in under the slab he's got several of them lying, he did have more but one day when the tide was high during a storm it washed away most of them, so now he hasn't got very many he says, only a few left, well, one of the boat back home he's still got says Lars, and he asks me if I want to see a picture he has made of the boat back home and I nod and Lars crouches down on all fours and creeps under the slab and it's dark and I can only catch a glimpse of him and Lars comes creeping out again and stands up and hands me yet another piece of driftwood and I can see that he has painted both the mountains back home and our boat and it is not difficult to see what they represent in general and I think well, Lars is a clever brother.

Good, I say.

Yes, says Lars.

Do you make pictures when you stay away from home? I ask.

It does happen, replies Lars.

And I can hear that his voice sounds a tiny bit cross.

Now and again, he says.

And otherwise you walk around the island, I say.

At first I used to just walk round the island, he says.

And then you began to make those pictures? I say.

And Lars nods.

But it's only when you're like that that you want to make pictures? I say

and Lars nods again. And I look at the picture of the mountains back home and the boat and I can see that the picture looks a lot like Lars when he is that way, sure, it looks like the mountains back home and our boat, but otherwise it looks most like Lars when he is that way, as he is now and again. I think it is strange to see how the picture reminds one of Lars when he's that way. It's black in the same way as Lars is black. The darkness is the same. It's a darkness that is not dead, but which shines, a shining darkness, kind of.

The picture looks like you, I say.

Lars looks suddenly at me.

How do you mean? he says.

No, I don't know.

But there is a likeness, I say.

Shall I make a picture of you? asks Lars.

And I don't really want anyone making a picture of me, no, I don't want that. I shake my head.

I've already made a picture of you, says Lars.

And if he, Lars, has already made a picture of me, it's not something I can stop him doing, he's done it already, so he's done so already. Nothing to be done about that.

I can go and get the picture, says Lars.

And I can hear how glad Lars is by his voice and I see him crouch down on all fours and creep in under the slab, little by little under the slab he creeps and now I can barely see Lars, and only his feet clearly, and now Lars can be seen more and more and Lars gets up and hands me a piece of driftwood and I see a face looking up at an angle, with rather a large nose, with a rather crooked mouth, and with big eyes. And Lars has said it's me he has painted. But the picture doesn't look like me. Surely I don't look like that? But I can hardly tell Lars I don't look like that.

You don't look like that, says Lars

and he begins to laugh and collects up the pieces of driftwood and puts them together and then goes to the edge of the water. I can see Lars looking out over the sea and he lifts up a piece of driftwood in the air and throws it out to sea.

Don't throw away the pictures, I say.

And he, Lars, throws the other pieces of driftwood in one single cast and then comes running toward me and Lars runs past me and I can see Lars climbing up the rocks and I understand nothing and I don't know what to do and I hadn't said anything, but he still went and threw away his pictures because of me, so there must have been something, I think, and that everything had to go so wrong, that no one can be straightforward, I think, and climb up the rocks and get up onto the heights and go down the rocks to the beach and run along the beach and run up the path to our house and a couple of slates are leaning along the house wall and I look up and I see Father standing on the roof cursing, hell and damnation, he is saying, hell and damnation, go to hell, he says and drops a slate down onto the hill and it remains sticking up out of the ground and Father looks at me.

No, keep away, you! cries Father.

Be careful! Look out! shouts Father

and I see Mother come to the door and she is holding a baby under each arm and Elizabeth is clinging to her feet and Mother looks at me and shakes her head in resignation. I stop. I see Father standing on the roof of the house still holding another slate and is shouting loudly keep away and he lets go of the slate and the slate slides down the roof and flies off and reaches the soft ground and I see the slate sticking up crookedly out of the ground and I can see Mother in the doorway of our little house and hear her begin to weep. Father is standing on the roof looking at me.

Now we're going to move, Father shouts.

Now it's enough, Father shouts at me.

When they start throwing stones at people's house wall, then you've had enough, he shouts.

You understand, he says.

I nod.

I'm going to knock down the house and build it up again with my own hands, he says.

I've built this house and I shall knock it down and build it up again, he says.

What shall we do with the plot of land, I ask.

They can have that, as thanks for throwing stones, says Father.

They can have it, he says.

They can do what they want with the earth, he says.

They can have the earth! shouts Father

and I can see that he is almost losing his balance as he stands there on the roof of the house and he falls to one side and grips the ridgepole and I see Mother coming towards me with one child under each arm and I can see her crying quietly and says this must be God's will, you must not defy God's plan for us, she says to me and I see Father stand up on the roof and I can hear my little sister Elizabeth howling Father, Father! Father be careful! And I see Father work loose another slate and he lets go of the slate and it slides down the roof and it falls off and hits another slate and both slates snap in two and I hear Father shouting hell! hell! shouts Father and Mother shouts that he shouldn't swear so and where has Lars got to? asks Mother and so the two little ones Mother has under her arms begin to cry.

Calm down now, says Mother

and she looks up at Father.

Come down from there, you don't need to knock down the whole house right now, says Mother.

Yes I do, says Father

and I see him sit down on the roof and move slowly down the roof, toward the ladder, and he gets onto the ladder, climbs down. Father walks over to us.

I think you can travel to Stavanger right away, you can stay with my brother, he says

and he says he can then follow with the house, they can take a small cargo boat, says Father.

Yes, says Mother.

And I can see that Mother's eyes are moist.

But so suddenly, she says.

Yes, so suddenly, says Father

and he goes and stacks the slates he has thrown along the house wall next to the other slates stacked along the house wall.

It's going to rain, says Mother.

It's going to rain in, she says.

Do you understand? she says

and Mother looks at Father and he says then damn it it'll just have to rain in, tomorrow she can take the kids with her and travel to Stavanger, he'll book a berth on the boat, he's thought it all out already he says and Mother says yes yes and I look out at the beach and see that the sea has grown black again and see that the sky is completely black now and I feel the first of the rain.

It's beginning to rain, says Mother.

You'll have to take the kids inside, says Father.

Where's Lars, asks Father

and looks at me. I shake my head.

That that boy will keep on running around the island, I don't understand it, he says.

Our eldest son, we could do with a bit of help from him, with all those kids to feed, he says.

I see Mother go inside, with a child under each arm and I see my little sister Elizabeth rush in after her. And suddenly it starts to rain hard, I notice the rain coming down in full force, and then comes the wind, the wind comes nearly as suddenly, the wind comes in from the sea with great force and Father says that if he had known it was going to be weather like this he wouldn't have started taking the slates off the roof, and how could anyone have known? just now the sun was shining, says Father and he had better carry on, he can't just take some slates off the roof, it looks too crazy, he says, no, now I must carry on, he says and climbs up the ladder again, in the pouring rain he climbs up the

ladder, and the wind tugs at the ladder, while Father is climbing
it tugs at the ladder, and I can see that the ladder is coming away,
and I rush over and take hold of the ladder and Father looks down
at me and says thank you, thanks, Oline he says and I can now
see the wind tugging at the ladder and it is raining really hard and
I look down towards the beach and I can see Lars standing down
there by the beach bringing in the boat, out to sea in such weather, what is he thinking of, the lunatic, why? why does he want to
go out to sea in such weather, I am thinking, and see Lars climb
aboard the boat and it bobs up and down on the waves that have
become pretty big by now, and he mustn't row out too far when
the weather's like this, I am thinking and look up at Father who
has just put one foot onto the roof, the other foot is on the top
rung of the ladder and Father pushes the ladder aside and I push
against it and I can see Lars sit down on the thwart and put out
the oars and he tries to row against the breakers and the boat is
hardly moving forward at all, is barely making any headway, and
I can see Lars rowing for all he's worth, and I look up and cannot
see Father, he has got onto the roof now, I think, and Lars should
not be rowing on the sea in this weather, I will have to run down
and get him back, he can't row out when it's blowing like this, I
think, and I let go of the ladder and in the rain and in the wind I
go to the path and turn around and can see Father straddling the
ridge and he is loosening a slate up on the roof and I can see the
wind tugging at the ladder and I now see that the ladder had slid
a little to one side and a strong gust of wind shakes the ladder and
I see the ladder crash to the ground and Father sitting there on
the ridge and it looks as if he hasn't even noticed the ladder has
fallen to the ground and I can see Lars has rowed some distance
from land and he mustn't row out to sea in such weather, I am
thinking, and I start to run down the path towards the beach, I
must get Lars to row back to land again, I think, and I run down
the path, through all the rain, through the wind I run, and I get
down to the beach and I see Lars sitting out there in the boat and
rowing for all he's worth and the boat is hardly moving forward.

You must come back in Lars, I cry.

You mustn't row out in such weather, I cry.

You mustn't Lars!

Come back in, Lars!

You mustn't! I cry

and see Lars lifting the oars out of the sea and a large breaker brings the boat quite a distance toward land, a new breaker takes the boat even nearer to land.

Father's knocking down the house! I cry.

Look Lars, he's taking the slates from the roof! I shout

and Lars looks at the roof of the house and I hear him begin to laugh out loud and then he puts out the oars again and tries to turn the boat around and succeeds and then takes the boat rapidly landward and Lars stows the oars in the boat then he jumps up in the boat stands on the prow and the boat rocks up and down, up and down, and Lars stands with his one foot over the gunwale of the boat ready to take the thud as the boat hits the shore and the boat is gliding toward land and Father shouts that it would be a pity, the boat could get smashed up, the boat could break up and Lars takes the boat in smoothly and Father shouts that that would be a pity, if the boat had got smashed and Lars holds and moors the boat and it is raining and raining, it is pouring down, and now it is raining and raining, without end, and I am wet through and the wind feels cold and I can see that the boat is moored and Lars is standing down on the beach by the boat.

Come on Lars, I say.

Lars turns around toward me.

Come on, I say

and Lars walks toward me.

We're going home now, I say.

Lars nods.

The weather suddenly got stormy, he says.

Such things happen, here on the island, I say.

Very changeable, he says.

I begin to walk up the path and Lars walks alongside.

Neither you nor I are christened, I say.

Nearly everyone else is christened.

And since we're not christened, we can't get confirmed either, I say.

Father doesn't like clergymen, says Lars.

No, I say.

But nearly everyone else is christened or confirmed, and I've heard it's hard to get a job if you're neither christened nor confirmed, I say.

Do you believe that?

Yes, I say.

I've thought about getting christened and confirmed, I say.

Lars nods.

We'll no doubt be moving to Stavanger.

We can surely get christened and confirmed in Stavanger, I say.

Maybe, says Lars.

I'm going to, anyway, I say.

I might do so too, says Lars.

We walk up the path.

But that Father should take down the roof in such weather, says Lars.

He says it's because one of the neighbors has thrown a stone at the house, I say

and I look at Lars and can see him nodding.

You didn't tell him it was me? says Lars.

I shake my head and Lars and I walk up the path toward our house.

The ladder seems to have fallen down, I say.

I'll have to put it up again, says Lars

and we carry on toward our house and Lars then goes and picks up the ladder, he swings it upward and the wind catches the ladder and jerks it from side to side and Lars leans the ladder against the wall of the house and I can see Lars beginning to climb up it up toward the roof and in such a wind! it's very likely to fall down! and I run over to the ladder and take hold of it and there I am holding the ladder firmly and I can see Lars climbing up to the roof and I hear Lars say to Father is he trying to take down the roof in this weather and I hear Father say that we're going to be moving house, you can't live here anymore, he says, we're now going to move into Stavanger town, he says, it can't get any worse than here and we're going to take the house with us, we will put it up again in Stavanger town, says Father and Lars asks if he can help and Father says that would be nice, I could do with a helping hand he says and watches Lars climb up onto the roof and I just can't see him anymore and this is almost too crazy, why should Father set about taking down the roof when it is raining and blowing so much and Lars doesn't seem to think it is odd to take down the slates from the roof in this weather, he asked Father for once whether he could help Father, and this has hardly ever happened before, if at all? as far as I can remember it has not happened, I think, and I can't just stand here holding the ladder because I'm frozen to the bone and am wet through, and the wind is cold and hard, and I've now told Lars that I've thought about getting christened and confirmed and it looks as if Lars could think of doing so too, maybe he thinks that if he is going to be painting pictures he will have to get christened and confirmed like other people, that's maybe what he thinks, is what I'm thinking, and I let go of the ladder and walk some little way away from the house and can now see both Father and Lars sitting up there athwart the ridge of the roof. They are sitting athwart the ridge of the roof, facing each other.

I'm freezing so much, I can't keep hold of the ladder any longer, I shout.

And neither Father nor Lars seem to hear that I am calling out to them and I call out again and can see Lars turning towards me.

I'm going inside, I shout.

Lars nods.

The ladder will fall down, do you want to come down, are you going to be hammering on the roof, I shout.

Yes, yes, shouts Father

and I see Father let go of another slate, it skids down the roof, flies off and I see the slate hit the ground and stick up crooked out of the ground. I can see that soon the whole top row of slates will have been removed. I am freezing. I go inside and hear kids shrieking, there is always the yelling of kids, everywhere and always is there the yelling of small kids, and I can see pools of water on the floor and I can see that it is dripping from the ceiling and Mother sitting in a corner holding onto one child under each arm and down by her feet are sitting Elizabeth and Cecilia and I can see Mother sitting there crying quietly. I can see Mother and she can't just sit there crying in the privy, thinks Oline, and she can't just sit here in the privy and remember and become like a child all over again, thinks Oline. But Mother sat there weeping. And the morning after the floor was covered with water. And Oline thinks she will have to get up and go now, she can't keep on sitting there in the privy, her legs are no longer aching either, she will have to stand up and go into the kitchen with the fish, because it is cold, she is freezing, she can't just sit there in the privy either, thinks Oline, but has anything come out? no she doesn't think so and she's been sitting here quite some time, but nothing has come out, that she knows, well a little has come out and in her drawers too, not very much, but a little bit, thinks Oline, now she will have to get a grip on herself, she thinks, and now she will have to take the fish into the kitchen but since it's so cold in there she'll have to light the stove, and there's still a little water, her grandchildren are capable of doing so, they go and fetch some for her, not that it is so far to go and fetch water, but this is what she has become, everything needs effort now, even going out to the privy requires effort, everything has become an effort, everything is a challenge, even if she walks the smallest distance her feet begin to ache, that's what it's become like and hardest of all is fetching water, that's such a struggle, and she can only manage because of her grandchildren, they are good, they fetch her water, without them, well, well, her grandchildren, yes, children and grandchildren. But now she really will have to stand up. She can't stay sitting like that, thinks Oline and she presses her hands on the edge of the toilet seat and she pushes herself up from the edge of the toilet seat and she gets hold of her drawers and pulls them up and can see that they don't look completely clean, no and wet too, and she pulls her drawers up halfway up her thighs, and she puts her one foot on the floor, then the other, and so Oline is standing with both feet on the floor and with her backside halfway off the edge of the toilet and Oline takes hold of her stick and placing her full weight on the stick she pushes herself onto her feet with all her might, leaning forward, leaning forward on her stick, with her face downward, and she looks at the fish on the hook on the door.

Fish and fish, says Oline.

Without the fish we would have been in a mess, says Oline. We must have fish, she says.

Less appetite though, but you've got to get something down you, got to eat something, says Oline

and with her free hand she lifts the string with the fish off the hook on the door and lifts the hook and shuffles to the door and opens it a little. Oline peeks out. And Oline sees that it has begun to rain a little, but only a few drops. Oline gathers her strength, she notices that her feet are stiff, almost lifeless they feel, she is thinking and Oline tries to set her body in motion, and she puts one foot forward, then the other. And Oline leaves the privy. With her stick in one hand, and the fish in the other, she leaves the privy. Oline moves toward her house. Now she will go straight into the kitchen, gut the fish, make it ready for boiling, then get the fire going in the stove, sit down and do a bit of knitting or crocheting. That's what she's going to do, yes, thinks Oline and she opens the red door to her nice little house, with the hand she is holding the fish in she opens the nice red door, and she enters her house, and Oline looks at the flagstones of the floor in the hall and she can see their Father sitting astride the roof ridge there on Borgøya and Father is letting go of slate after slate so they fall to the ground and stick crookedly out of it, Father, Father, Oline thinks and now she thinks she mustn't lose herself in reveries again, Oline must go straight into the kitchen and gut and wash the fish and then sit down, because the ache is coming back again so she must sit herself down, thinks Oline and she goes into the kitchen and puts the fish on the table, and she sits herself down at the table, and she leans her stick against the edge of the table, and she puts the chopping board in front of her, takes the knife out of its sheath, she picks up the one fish and feels that it is dry and a little sticky, her fingers stick to the fish, and Oline cuts the head off the one fish. She sees that the blood has clotted. She cuts the head off the other fish. She sees the two fish heads lying next to one another, attached to the string. She guts the one fish. She guts the other fish. She gets to her feet, takes the fish and unsteadily, because she has to walk without her stick, Oline goes to the kitchen counter and as long as she doesn't fall, thinks Oline, I mustn't fall down now, thinks Oline, and Oline walks unsupported over to the kitchen counter and Oline puts them in a bowl that is standing on the kitchen counter and takes a mug and gets some water, pours the water over the fish and Oline is walking carefully, carefully, on unsteady legs back to the table and she takes down a plate from the cupboard above the table and she slides the fish heads onto the plate. And Oline takes her stick, she's got to go out again, she thinks, you can never get any peace, now she has to go out again with the guts, and doesn't it feel as if she needs to go again? Isn't it pressing down there? yes she surely needs to go? or not? yes, she does, that's what it feels like, thinks Oline and leaning on her stick, and with the plate with the guts in her other hand, Oline leaves her house, and down there on the road she can see someone coming, oh if only she can manage to see who it is, but now! a few years ago she would have seen easily who it was, thinks Oline, but now! she has to bend down and put down the plate, for the cats! for the gulls! for anyone who wants the guts, she must put down the plate, thinks Oline, but it's difficult to bend down, but it must be done, it must be done, thinks Oline and she sees the person is approaching and Oline hears them saying, well, the cat has to have what it deserves, and Oline hears from her voice that it is Alida who is walking up to her. Well, well, if it isn't Alida. No, it'll be pleasant to have a few words with Alida, thinks Oline. Alida, yes, Alida.

The cat has to have what it deserves, yes, says Oline

and she sees Alida stop right in front of her.

You don't want to come in and have a cup of coffee, says Oline

and Alida says yes I do, a cup of coffee would taste nice, and she's not in a hurry to do anything, and for all she knows that's why she had a little walk as well, to have a drop of coffee, says Alida and laughs.

Oh, Alida, Alida, says Oline.

You can come in then, says Oline.

Aren't you going to put out those guts? says Alida.

I usually throw them onto the ground, by the privy, says
Oline

and she thinks oh no! oh no! for all those years she has done
just that, gone out with the guts, thrown them onto the ground
for the gulls, for the cat, it always vanishes anyway, and today she
had the idea that she could put it out by the front door, on a plate.
Things are beginning to go really wrong with her, thinks Oline.

Shall I throw them away for you? asks Alida.

No, I'll just have to manage myself, says Oline

and she'll just have to manage like this, thinks Oline, my
feet will just have to ache and ache like this, she must manage to
throw away the guts herself and Oline gathers her strength and
with her back bent, and slowly, step by step, she walks over to the
privy, and Oline thinks that she should have gone to the privy
already, because something is pressing, she will have to go, she
thinks, but not just now! not just now that Alida has come for
a visit, she can't just go and sit there on the privy, thinks Oline,
and she is holding the plate with the guts out in front of her and
she sees the fish heads lying next to one another on the grass and
she sees some of the guts stuck to the plate and Oline takes hold
of the guts and they stick to her fingers and she tries to throw it
away and some of it loosens then she shakes her fingers a little bit
more and it falls off and then she goes and wipes her fingers across
the plate and she shakes her fingers and wipes them on her skirt.
Oline turns around and walks toward Alida.

It's worse getting old than you could have imagined, says
Oline.

It's much worse, she says.

It's shit getting old, says Oline

and her feet ache again and she says oh.

You're in pain, says Alida.

It's my feet, says Oline.

Yes, my feet, she says.

It's my feet that are aching.

It's worst when I walk, when I sit down it isn't so bad, she says.

But you can manage, says Alida

and Oline sees that the door to her house is standing open and she and Alida go inside.

Yes, your house got really nice once it was painted, says Alida.

White house, red door, she says

and Alida shuts the door behind her. And Oline goes into the kitchen.

We can put on the coffee then, says Oline

And Alida comes walking into the kitchen.

I might as well do that, says Alida.

Yes thanks, maybe, yes thanks, says Oline.

I'll go into the room and sit down for a bit, she says.

You do that, says Alida.

And Oline goes into the room and she thinks that Alida, she's known Alida all her days, but now she is beginning to forget everything, so that she is not sure anymore who this Alida is, but she must know Alida. Alida knows where her coffee is, and she must know the house pretty well. No, this is just too much. This is becoming crazy. She must know who this Alida is. But she mustn't go and say anything that would suggest that she doesn't know who Alida is, she does know, she's known Alida all these years, but to remember who she might be, it's that that is so hard. She must remember who Alida is, thinks Oline. She remembers so much, so she must remember who this Alida is, thinks Oline, and she goes and sits down on her chair. And Oline feels how good it is to sit down, it's as if a heavy peace is moving bit by bit through her body and removes the pain and makes her feel more and more peaceful.

It was nice to be able to sit down, says Oline.

That it can be so nice to sit down, she says

and she can hear Alida bustling about out there in the kitchen and Alida calls out that the coffee will soon be ready.

That'll be nice, says Oline.

Yes, it's a bit cold in your house, a little something warm inside you will do you good, Alida says from out in the kitchen

and Oline sees Alida coming into the room with two cups,

she puts them down on the table in front of her and Alida says that soon the coffee will be ready, she says, so you can have a drop, and then they can talk a bit as they used to do, says Alida.

Yes, okay, says Oline.

About the old days, says Alida

and she laughs briefly and Oline thinks that Alida has always had the habit of saying something and then giving a little laugh like that, Alida says something, and then she laughs briefly.

Yes, okay, says Oline

and she can see Alida go out into the kitchen again and Oline thinks that she and Alida certainly have lots to talk about, by what Alida just said, thinks Oline, and she can see Alida standing in the window, in a little house down by the sea Alida is standing in the window and she is calling from the window and is asking whether Oline can't drop in for a chat and Oline says I can, I don't have to go home yet to make dinner, I say and I go up to the house and I see Lars trotting down to the sea, on those short legs of his, with his long back, Lars never walks like anyone else, nor does he run, he neither walks nor runs, he trots all the time, and I can see his big beard lying to one side from the speed and his eyes are brown and today his eyes look quite calm, under the black brim his eyes look quite calm, in their brownness, and his long black hair is swept backwards, lifting in the wind. And over his shoulder a saw is hanging. A bucksaw, as Lars would say. The best saw, he always says. I see Lars coming trotting along, with the bucksaw over his shoulder. And now Lars will find someone to saw firewood for. Lars saws wood for people. He gets a cup of coffee and a little money for the work. Now Lars is outside sawing firewood for someone who needs a little firewood sawn up. And Lars sees me and his face opens up in a smile behind his big black beard.

You're going to saw some firewood, I say.

Yes, that's right, says Lars

and he stops in front of me, he's a little out of breath, he's been hurrying so much.

If anyone needs any firewood sawing, he says.

Yes, that's always needed, he says.

And you've gone and got some fish, he says.

Yes, I have, I say.

Maybe you need someone to saw up firewood for you, says Lars.

No, I'm all right for firewood right now, I say.

But maybe Alida needs some, she asked me to come in for a chat, I can ask her, I say

and Lars says that would be fine, Alida will no doubt need a little firewood sawn up, because it's a long time since he's sawn up firewood for her, says Lars, if she needs a little firewood sawn up, he says.

We can go to Alida's, and we can ask her, I say.

Lars nods and I notice that he's hesitating a bit.

Yes, you can follow along, I say.

Your big sister will look after you, I say.

Right then, says Lars

and he laughs and then Lars and I go inside Alida's house, into the kitchen, and when Alida sees Lars standing there with the bucksaw, as he says, over his shoulder, she says well Lars that would be nice, I need a little firewood, sure I do, says Alida and Lars says that was just what he was thinking, because it's a long time since he's been there to saw firewood for Alida, he says.

Yes, it's been a long time now, says Alida.

I nearly thought that you wouldn't come again, she says.

There's been a lot of work to do, says Lars.

No doubt, says Alida.

But now I've hardly got any sawn up firewood, says Alida.

So it's a good thing I've come, says Lars.

Yes, as if I'd asked you, says Alida.

Yes, you know, says Lars.

You really are one, Lars, I say.

Yes, yes, says Lars

and I notice that his voice has changed in some way, and Alida must also have noticed this, because she now says how really nice it is that Lars has come, and she's just been making coffee so if he wants he can have a drop before doing his job today too and not just afterwards as he usually does, says Alida, and Lars shakes his head and I can see his eyes darkening and he gets a little of that black shine in his eyes.

Only if you want to, says Alida.

Or we can do what we usually do, first the sawing, then you get a cup of coffee afterwards, says Alida.

Yes, it's better that it stays as it's always been, I say.

Yes, yes, says Lars.

Because the serpent is writhing, he says.

Yes, you're right there, says Alida.

I know the snake is writhing, I've seen it with my own eyes, says Lars

and he stands there with his short legs, with his long back, and I can see him staring down.

Yes, you know best, Lars, I say.

And they've no idea about art, says Lars.

Not the least thing, he says.

They know no more about art than a calf's backside, he says.

Not one bit more, says Lars

and Lars is standing in Alida's kitchen and looking down at the floor and I can hear his voice quaking and Alida and I exchange glances.

They don't understand art, says Lars.

And not all artists should be killed, he says.

But nearly all of them should, not all, but nearly all, he says.

I can see Alida standing looking at me and shaking her head in resignation. And Lars is standing there in her kitchen and staring down at the floor.

I'll kill nearly every painter, he says.

They must be killed, they can't paint and therefore they must be killed, he says.

Yes, yes, I say.

I really will kill them, says Lars.

But wouldn't you like a drop of coffee? says Alida.

Kill them, yes, says Lars.

Alida's asking if you would like a little coffee, I say

and I can see Lars standing there staring down at the floor and I look at Alida and she looks at me.

You could have a little coffee, says Alida
and Lars looks up and at Alida.
Yes please, I'd really like a little coffee, says Lars.
It would taste nice, yes, he says.
Just sit yourself down, then, says Alida.
Yes, thank you, thank you, says Lars.
And then afterwards I'll saw up all the firewood you need,
he says.
Good on you, Lars, says Alida.
A little coffee first, I say.
Yes, that's right, says Lars
and I see Lars go and sit down at Alida's kitchen table.
Well, well, Lars, says Alida.
No one saws as fast or as well as you do, she says.
Not to mention painting, no one paints like you do, she says.
That's how it is, says Lars.
And Alida goes and fetches a cup that she places in front of
Lars and she pours out the coffee for him and I see Lars pick up
his pipe, the big curved pipe, and he stops his pipe, and he does so
thoroughly, slowly, and he fills his pipe with tobacco, slowly, thoroughly, and Lars strikes a match and the flame flares up and Lars
sucks until the flame bends and goes down into the pipe and Lars
tamps and tamps and the good sharp smell of the smoke spreads
around Alida's kitchen and Alida tells me to sit down and I sit
down opposite Lars and Alida brings two cups and she puts one
down in front of me and the other by the empty place next to me
and Alida pours out the coffee, first for me, then for herself, and
I watch Lars sitting there and stopping his pipe and Lars lifts the
cup to his lips and slurps the warm coffee.
Good coffee, good, says Lars
A good pipe and a good cup of coffee, says Lars
and Oline hears Alida saying that now the coffee is ready,
now there'll be coffee, says Alida and Oline looks up and sees Alida standing there in the doorway of her kitchen looking at her.
I was thinking about Lars, says Oline.
Yes, Lars, says Alida.
I was thinking about one time down at your house, he came

to saw up firewood, as he used to, and afterwards would drink some coffee, but on that occasion you gave him his coffee beforehand as well, before he went off to do his sawing, says Oline.

It was the time that while we were drinking coffee he stood up suddenly and ran out, says Alida.

Yes, yes, says Oline.

He just ran off, says Oline.

And that day he had talked so horribly about killing all painters, so we didn't know what to believe, says Alida.

Yes, I remember, says Oline.

But he came back, says Alida.

Yes, he did, oh yes, she says.

Sure he came back, yes, says Oline.

Sure he did, says Alida.

And then he sawed a lot of firewood, and so quickly, I've never seen anything like it, she says.

Yes, he was something special, Lars was, says Oline.

Yes, you said it, says Alida.

But now the coffee is ready, says Alida

and Oline sees Alida go out again into the kitchen and she sees her come in again with cups and she puts the cups down, one in front of Oline, one at the place opposite her, and Oline now thinks that she must try to remember who this Alida is, she knows her so well, she has been so often down at her place, in her house, down by the sea, now all she has to do is recall who this Alida is, it can't have got so far that she doesn't know who Alida is, soon she won't know who she is herself either, when it's got as far as that, who is she herself? what are her children called? her grandchildren? what has she done all her life? no, that would be a horrible question, thinks Oline, and she thinks that even if she doesn't know who she herself is, she could at least manage to work out who this Alida is, she does know, she remembers so well that day many years ago when Alida and she herself and Lars were in Alida's kitchen drinking coffee, the day Lars stood up from the table and ran out leaving a half-drunk cup of coffee, he ran out just like that, she remembers that, she can see it before her eyes, as if it were happening right now, she can see Lars sitting opposite her

at the table in Alida's kitchen staring down at the table, then it is
as if his gaze fastens on something and then I hear his feet beginning to tramp and his feet tramp rapidly up and down, and his
gaze has fastened on something and the cup is standing in front
of him on the table and I can see the twitching around his eyes
and can see his eyes become moist and it is as if his gaze is still fastened on something, it is quite fixed, it doesn't let itself be pulled
away from what it was fixed on, and his feet tramp, and his eyes
get moister and then there are violent twitches around his eyes
and I can see Lars tear himself loose, with all his might, Lars is
gathering his strength, tears himself loose with all his might and I
see him cross the floor and run out and me and Alida look at one
another and Oline hears Alida calling from the kitchen that the
coffee is on its way, the coffee's ready, calls Alida and Oline sees
Alida coming in with the kettle and Oline thinks she must calm
down, now she really has to remember who this Alida is, who is
this Alida? is she married to her brother, is that how it stands? and
Alida is old but not as old as her, thinks Oline and Oline thinks
that strictly speaking this is something to laugh at, nothing more,
would she have thought some years ago that one day she wouldn't
be able to remember who Alida is, thinks Oline, and she hears Alida say that coffee's ready, yes she is pouring the coffee for Oline
and she sees Alida pour coffee into the other cup too.

Aren't you going to ask about your brother? says Alida

and Oline thinks, ah, to think that she hadn't thought of it
right away that Alida is married to her brother. And it's not Alida who's married to Sivert. It's Signe who's married to Sivert. And
didn't Signe ask her to come to visit her, hadn't Sivert asked to talk
with her? Wasn't that what happened? Or maybe it was Alida who
asked, and now Alida has come up to fetch her?

Well, there's not much news about your brother for the time
being, says Alida.

Unchanged, yes, says Oline

and she thinks, yes, that's how it is, Alida is married to her
brother, and they've had many children as well, but now her brother is old and poorly, just like she is, that's how it is, yes, thinks
Oline.

Yes, says Alida

and she sighs and Oline thinks that she must ask if he hasn't got any better, if he's got worse, she'll have to ask something like that, thinks Oline.

Unchanged, yes, says Oline

and she sees Alida go out into the kitchen with the kettle and come back and sit down opposite her at the table, and now things are pressing down there again, she needs to go, now it really is pressing, thinks Oline, as long as it doesn't come out by itself, thinks Oline, she did sit for a long time in the privy just now, she even took the fish into the privy with her, thinks Oline, that she did, thinks Oline, and now it's pressing pretty badly but now nothing must come out, at least not at the back, if anything comes out it should come out at the front, and has something come out? is something happening down there, thinks Oline, and just think that it would end up like this with her, thinks Oline, no, that it should end like this, who would have thought it, thinks Oline, and she hears Alida say that it's just the same with your brother, no news, he's got problems feeding himself, and he's never been clear in his head, Alida says and laughs.

No, no, he hasn't, says Oline.

And Alida begins to laugh.

No, he's always been a bit special, says Oline.

Those Quakers are all a bit special, says Alida.

There have been quarrels about everything.

He didn't want to join the army, and the kids weren't to be christened, she says.

We weren't to get married, she says.

And now he doesn't want to get decently buried either, says Alida.

Yes, that's how it is, says Oline.

Couldn't they be like other people, says Alida.

Yes, couldn't they, says Oline.

But no, they can't, says Alida.

And Lars became completely nutty, he did, she says.

It was bad enough with the rest of them, but Lars was worst of all, she says.

But you shouldn't speak ill of the dead, I'll have to watch my mouth, says Alida.

Lars, yes, says Oline.

He who was sent to school and all that, says Alida.

He could have become a great man, she says.

Yes, says Oline.

But he got sick, poor guy, says Alida.

Yes, he did, says Oline.

He could have become really important, but I suppose it ended as it had to, says Alida.

How's it with your aches and pains? she says

and Oline says that if she can only sit and rest, then it doesn't ache, only if she walks then it aches, she says, but she has to walk, she says, she can't just stay sitting down, that would never do, she can't just give up, that's not possible, she has to go out to fetch fish every day, says Oline and Alida says no, you can't just give up, is what she says, no they can't, as long as their feet carry them they must keep on walking, says Alida and Oline hears Alida say that the coffee tasted good, it's always nice to have a cup of coffee, says Alida.

Coffee, yes, says Oline.

Nice to have a cup of coffee, she says.

Became good and strong, it did, says Oline.

The coffee was good, says Alida.

Sad that your husband is so sick, says Oline.

Yes, yes, says Alida.

That he should be at death's door, that's horrible, says Oline and suddenly Alida looks Oline straight in the face.

No he's not at death's door, says Alida

and Oline thinks didn't Alida say just now that he was at death's door, that she, Oline, would have to go and visit Alida at home, because her brother had said to Alida that he wanted to have a word with her before he passed away, wasn't that what Alida had said just now?

No, he's not at death's door, says Alida.

And didn't Alida, thinks Oline, ask her to go along home with her, to talk with her brother when she went down to the sea for fish, wasn't it Alida who stuck her head out of the window and asked if she didn't want to come in and talk to her brother, with Sivert, yes, that's it, and they had better go and talk to Sivert too then, so he doesn't pass away before they get there, they can't just sit here drinking coffee, no that would never do.

Sivert, yes, says Oline.

Yes, Sivert, he's pretty bad now, says Alida.

He's probably at death's door, says Oline.

Really? says Alida.

Yes, yes, says Oline.

No, I didn't know that, says Alida.

That's horrible, she says.

Is it Signe that told you? says Alida

and sure it was Signe who told her, thinks Oline, and now they had better get up and go there before Sivert dies, he's lying there and wants to speak with her, so they'll have to go, they can't just sit there drinking coffee while Sivert is lying there dying and really wants to talk to his big sister before he goes, no that would never do.

We should go soon, says Oline.

Go? says Alida.

We really should, says Oline.

Where, then? says Alida.

To talk to Sivert, says Oline.

Shouldn't we just leave him in peace? says Alida

and Oline thinks that she now saw it clearly, no, that it should all end like this with her, because it isn't Alida who is married to Sivert, and she, Alida, doesn't even know that Sivert is at death's door, but that she could get so mixed up! whatever has happened to her! she can't remember, can hardly see, her feet ache, how has it come to this, thinks Oline, and she can't hold her water, and hardly her number twos either, oh dear, thinks Oline.

Yes, yes, says Oline.

I can see that the floor isn't completely clean in the kitchen, says Alida.

Alida's always been like that, thinks Oline, has always thought that she is the messy one, as she puts it, always like that.

I can give it a once-over for you says Alida.

I can do that, she says.

It'll be done in a trice, says Alida.

I can do it myself, says Oline.

No, you're so bad on your feet, says Alida.

You could do with a bit of help, she says.

I'm still healthy enough, I can do your floor for you, says Alida.

Yes, yes, all right, if you really say so, says Oline

and she sees Alida empty her cup, and Alida gets to her feet, and Oline hears Alida say that she'll find some water and a washrag and give the floor a clean right away, she says.

Oline nods.

Yes, if you want to, says Oline

and Oline watches Alida go into the kitchen again and Alida has always been like that, thinks Oline, she's never been satisfied with anything that she, Oline, has done, never, thinks Oline, and Alida is no doubt beginning to become dissatisfied with her and she'll be wiping up her filth next, thinks Oline, and that would be rather demeaning, she thinks, but has she any pride left? no, that she lets herself be insulted in that way, thinks Oline, it's got so far with her, thinks Oline and can hear Alida clattering and bustling about in her kitchen, and Oline wonders well, does she know where all the things are, does she know, and Alida has never been satisfied with her, never, nor has she been satisfied with her husband either, and not at all with Lars, how she laughed at Lars when he wasn't there, she was all nicey-nicey in his presence, but when he wasn't there she wouldn't be that nice, no. And Oline hears the washrag being used on the kitchen floor. And was Alida kind to Lars? no she wasn't, only while he was sawing wood for her, for a pittance and nothing would force Lars to saw firewood for her, but did he get anything back but laughter for thanks, he didn't. All he got was being laughed at, thinks Oline and Alida came and pulled me by the arm.

Come on now, now you can see Lars sawing firewood, said Alida

and she stood there laughing at me, she was grinning all over her face.

Lars is sawing away right now, come on, come along, then you can see how he does it, said Alida.

Come on, said Alida.

Don't you feel like it? she said.

Come along, it's a sight to see.

Come on, said Alida

and she pulled at the sleeve of my cardigan and I couldn't do anything else but go with her, as she was so keen, I had to go along with her, so I let Alida drag me into her room, and the window was open there, and outside the window I could hear Lars shouting, we'll get you, you damned Germans, and I could hear the ax hitting a log and heard Lars shouting, no you don't want to, you lump, you don't want to, but you will! shouted Lars and I heard the ax hit the log once again and I could see Alida standing behind the drape grinning and she whispered to me, you've got to come, you've really got to see how he's strutting about, whispered Alida as she stood there with a grin all over her face.

Come on, come on, Alida said softly

and I went over and stood behind Alida. I could now see Lars standing in front of a chopping block, he'd put aside the saw leaning it on the wall of the privy, he was now standing with an ax in one fist and he looked both wild and crazy.

That's the German over and done for, said Lars.

Now a Norwegian painter will get his comeuppance, oh yes, he said.

Now we'll find a Norwegian painter, my God we will, he said

and Lars picked up a log and placed it on the chopping block.

Now you're going to get it, you bastard, he said.

You're going to damn well get it now, he said.

Now it's the end, he said

and Lars raised the ax above his head and brought it down with all his might onto the log, and clove it in two so that the halves fell off the chopping block.

That's you done for, he said.

You were a bastard, a damn Norwegian painter, but now you're done for, he said.

I finished you off, I did, he said.

No doubt about it, I finished you off, no, he said.

It just had to happen, he said.

I knew I'd do away with you one fine day, said Lars.

You bastard!

You never could paint, never, but you still carried on and tormented those who could paint, you just had to do it, says Lars.

Bastard!

Here in Sandvigen, in Stavanger town, no bastards like you can live!

Not among ordinary folk, no way! says Lars

and I can see Lars pick up another log from the woodpile, he puts it on the chopping block, he lifts his ax.

You've got your comeuppance! shouts Lars

and Alida begins to snicker and holds her mouth too and she nudges me with her shoulder.

That's put paid to you, you miserable painter, says Lars.

That's justice for you, he says.

Justice.

Just as it should be, says Lars

and Alida whispers in my ear that Lars doesn't look quite clean, he should wash up, maybe I, his sister, can get him to do so, whispers Alida and I can hear Lars saying to himself that he ought now to do a bit of sawing, and he puts a dry piece of firewood in the groove of the sawhorse, picks up the saw, sets the saw in motion, and I go right up to the window.

Lars, how's it going, I call out.

Lars stops sawing, looks up at me.

It's going just fine, he says.

And how are you? he says.

Yes, better and better, I say.

You're both sawing and chopping wood, I say.

When I want to split logs, I split them, when I want to saw, I saw, says Lars.

I do what I want, he says.

Yes, you do, I say.

And Lars straightens up, turns around, looks around.

Yes, yes, he says.

On the beach, says Lars

and lifts his head, looks at me and asks if Alida wants two or four shillings' worth of firewood, and I move back from the window, I go into the room and can see Alida standing behind the drape, her hand over her mouth and I tell her that Lars wants to know whether she wants firewood for two or four shillings and Alida nods, for two, she says while she swiftly removes her hand from her mouth, before covering her mouth with her hand once again and I go over to the window and call out to Lars that she wants firewood for four shillings and Lars replies for four shillings and I see him bend over the sawhorse and the saw starts its work, going on, and on, and Oline sees Alida standing in the kitchen doorway.

Well, the kitchen floor's nice and clean now, she says.

And she, Alida's, always been like that, thinks Oline, she's always thought that she didn't keep the house clean enough, that she was a slut, and not good enough, thinks Oline and why is Alida bothering to do her floor, while her husband is lying there at death's door Alida is washing her floor, as if the floor were more important than her own husband, thinks Oline, and you just can't behave like that, thinks Oline. But saying something, thinks Oline, that just isn't done, thinks Oline. She had better keep her peace. She had better not say one word. It won't help anyway.

Shall I boil the fish for you? says Alida.

No I suppose I can boil it myself, says Oline.

Sure you can, says Alida.

But I can help you, you're bad on your legs, and I am after all here, says Alida.

Sure you're here, but I can manage to boil my own fish, says Oline.

Do you want any more coffee, in that case? says Alida.

No I've had enough, says Oline.

Well, then I think I'll be getting along home again, says Alida.

Yes, do that, says Oline.

Go home to your sick husband, she says.

He'll need your help, she says.

He can manage quite well on his own, says Alida.

He's not that helpless, says Alida.

But do go anyway, says Oline.

I'm a bit tired and think I'll have a little rest, says Oline.

Okay then, Oline, says Alida.

I'll be going now, says Alida

and then Oline says they can chat another time, and Alida nods and Alida leaves the room and enters the kitchen and Oline hears Alida shut the door behind her, and thinks that now at last Alida was here but now she's gone at last, why should Alida come here and disturb her? she had thought through what she was going to do, that she was going to light the stove, even that was something she was going to do, she was going to light the stove, make it warm and cosy, she had thought, and then she'd make herself some coffee, and then she'd sit down and knit or crochet, that's what she'd thought of doing, but then Alida came along and started washing the floor and now she must pop over to the privy, or maybe she should find her pot, because she maybe needs to go again, sure, a little bit at least, and she, Alida? she just can't remember who this Alida is either, more than the fact that Lars was at her place once and sawed up some wood, thinks Oline, and now is it pressing down there? does she need to go? and she'll have to drag herself out to the privy all over again, no, she doesn't want to do that, no, she'll have to make do with her pot, she'll just have to manage with her pot, she'll have to find her pot again, yes, yes, that she will have to manage, thinks Oline, and she takes hold of her walking stick and pushes herself to her feet and there Oline stands bent over her stick and she will just have to do a pee in the little room, poke the pot out from under the bed, then she'll have to take it into the big room and sit on the table as she usually does, thinks Oline, and she toddles across the floor, step by step, and sure enough her feet are aching again, thinks Oline, but she must move forward, all she has to do is move her feet the slightest bit, and the pain sets in, thinks Oline, but she'll have to move, go into the little room, because now it's pressing quite a lot down there.

Yes, yes, says Oline.

Getting old is real shit, she says.

Yes, yes, says Oline

and she draws the curtain to the little room aside and toddles into the little room and there the pot is standing, up on the
stool, that she has not even bothered to hide the pot under the
bed just seems too crazy, thinks Oline, and she takes the pot with
one hand and lifts it up and no, no, she hasn't emptied it for a
while she can see, and it's got that far with her, thinks Oline, no,
that it's got that far, that's horrible, thinks Oline, and the smell,
she shouldn't think about it, and her sense of smell isn't what it
was, and that's a good thing, thinks Oline, and she takes hold
of her stick and she puts it to the floor and presses against the
floor as she is bent over the stick, and she is holding the pot in
her hand. Oline begins to move, slowly, step by step Oline walks
bent forward, and it's aching and aching, and down there, at the
front, it's pressing and pressing, and there, no oh no, something's
coming out, not much, just a little, and it runs warm down her
thigh, Oline can feel, no, that things should have got this far with
her, thinks Oline, that she is beginning to piss herself, the water
comes just like that with no warning, she doesn't notice anything,
it just comes, thinks Oline, and goes over to the table and she
puts the pot on the table, at one end of the table stand two cups,
at the other stands the pot, Oline can see, and Oline lifts up her
skirts and she pulls down her drawers and sees that her drawers
are pretty wet, she sees, and not quite clean either, no, sees Oline,
she will have to change her drawers, wet as they are, thinks Oline
and she pulls down her drawers and takes hold of the edge of the
table with one hand and sits down on the pot, and with the other
hand puts it on her table, on her pot, in her room, and she sits on
it and grabs hold of the edge of the table, and Oline thinks that
something must come out now, she will just have to stay seated
for a long time, and she will have to sit and wait and see whether anything comes, thinks Oline, and isn't it also pressing there at
the back? isn't it pressing a bit? is something coming out? something had better come out soon, so that she doesn't have to sit up
there, on the pot, on the table, waiting for something to come
out, no this isn't right, this isn't how it should be, thinks Oline,

this isn't how it should be, thinks Oline, and that Alida should
come to her house, and she's known Alida for all these years, but
to remember who she is? who is this Alida, no, that's something
she can't remember, thinks Oline, that's something she'll just have
to remember, thinks Oline, and nothing is coming out either,
and she'll just have to stay put, now they should have seen her,
what if Alida saw her now, what if Alida should come rushing in
and see her sitting on her pot, no, she can't stay sitting like this
on her pot, no, she can't stay sitting like this, she will have to go
out to the privy, she would rather sit out there and not stay sitting
on her pot, up on the table in the room, thinks Oline, because
just imagine if someone came rushing in, she hasn't locked the
door, she hasn't thought that far, and she still hasn't lit the stove,
as she had thought of doing, she would light the stove at last, she
had thought, but hasn't done so yet, thinks Oline, and she had
thought she'd sit down and do a bit of knitting or crocheting, but
she hasn't done that, no, and it was surely Signe who told her that
Sivert wanted to talk to her, he was at death's door, said Signe, he
had asked Signe to ask her to come and talk with him, is what Sivert had said, and so she will have to go down to the sea again, but
her feet ache so, but if Sivert has asked her to talk with him, she
will have to go and talk with him, but as she's so confused it could
well have been something she's imagined, the fact that Sivert had
asked her to talk with him, thinks Oline, yes, yes. And now something must come out? she can't just sit there like that, up on her
pot, up on the table in the room, no that will never do. But now
she's sat down on the pot she'll just have to sit there thinks Oline,
she'll have to sit a little longer, she thinks, and she'll have to go
to see Sivert, because for sure Signe said that Sivert was at death's
door, and he asked after her, Signe said, he'd asked her to come
and talk with him, Signe did say that, thinks Oline, so she'd better
steel herself and go down to see Sivert, she thinks, there's no other
way, thinks Oline, no there isn't, she thinks, but something must
come out, thinks Oline and she sits on her pot while gripping the
edge of the table. No she can't go on sitting like this. And their
Father. And Lars who lived with Father, who stayed up in the attic when he wanted to do those daubs of his and would hang a

note on the door saying Do not disturb. When Lars hung a note on the door he wanted to paint. And then he would sit at the window under the ridge of the roof and look out. And he would do his daubs. Do not disturb, is what was written on the note. The attic where he would be while he painted. A short narrow bed. A chair. A chest in which he had his painting things and the finished pictures. There was a big lock on the chest. And Lars sitting there at the window looking out, his long black hair, his beard, his brown eyes, so mild, so wild. And Father who sat wriggling in his chair before he started talking about how the clergymen had taken God's word and name in vain forever and a day and made life unlivable for good people, and how the clergymen had sold cattle to honest folk only because they didn't want to do what the clergymen said and christen their children.

Those clergymen, said Father.

Those clergymen are not serving God, he said

Those clergymen can be regarded as swine, said Father

and he looked around him, his eyes wild, and he shook his head.

That not everyone becomes Quakers is something I just don't understand, says Father.

No, those clergymen, he says

and Lars and I look cautiously at one another, and we have decided together to get christened and confirmed and we've started taking confirmation classes, but neither of us have yet had the courage to tell Father.

What is needed is a rebellion, says Father.

Must put an end to it all, he says

and I see Lars get to his feet and I hear Father say to me that luckily he has never given in, it has cost him a lot to resist, cost him all kinds of creature comforts, says Father, but he hasn't given in.

Not one of my children have I had christened, says Father.

Not one.

Not one of the twelve have I had christened, he says.

I have not bowed to pressure, says Father.

No I have not, no, he says

and I think how I daren't tell him that I have thought of getting myself christened and confirmed, he'd take it very badly, I think to myself, Father will put up much resistance, he'll become furious, I think and hear Lars coming in again and can see Lars standing in the doorway across from me.

I'm going to get christened and confirmed, says Lars.

And Oline is too, he says.

I look at Father, he stays seated in his chair with his hands folded on his lap. And Father doesn't say anything. He shuts his eyes. Father is sitting with his hands on his lap and doesn't says a word. Father is sitting there, his eyes shut. Father doesn't say anything. Lars is standing in the doorway and he too isn't saying anything. I don't say anything. And I shut my eyes and fold my hands on my lap. And Lars comes and sits next to me, and we sit there, Father, Lars, and me. We sit in silence. We sit there for a long time. In the end Father gets up.

You will have to make up your own minds, he says

and Father leaves the room. Oline thinks oh no, no, she can't live in the past, she has to get a grip on herself, and she can't just sit there on her pot up on the table that she got once a long time ago and that she has always been so happy with, she can't stay sitting like that, on her pot, in her room, she mustn't, thinks Oline, and nothing has come out! yes it has, a little bit, yes, yes, a little bit, yes, yes, yes, and she should be satisfied, not so much has come out either, she has always been a modest eater all those days, all those years, and she has never started eating more, at least she doesn't eat a lot, she thinks, but she can't just sit there, on her pot, up on the table in the room, thinks Oline. No, that she can't. She will have to go, she thinks, to see Sivert.

I must go to see Sivert, says Oline.

I'm not mixing things up, it was Signe who asked me to come and talk with Sivert, says Oline.

I can't just sit like this, says Oline

and just think if someone should come and see her sitting on her pot, up there on the table, in the room, no that would be horrible, thinks Oline and right then there is a knock at the door. And Oline pushes herself up off her pot and pushes against the edge of the table and she is standing on the floor and her skirts fall down by themselves, but her drawers are hanging around her calves, and Oline can see the pot on the table, two cups and her pot on the table and near the edge of the table her stick is leaning, and Oline hears that again there is a knock at the door and she takes hold of her stick and takes a grip on the pot, and there is a shout, is there anybody there? is what is being shouted, wasn't that Signe's voice? and she will have to answer, thinks Oline and she looks toward the door to the room and she sees the door open and sees Signe standing there in the doorway.

No, ugh, says Signe.

No really, ugh, she says.

I shouldn't come rushing in like that, says Signe

and Oline stands there, leaning on her stick, with her pot in her other hand, and is looking down at the floor.

But your door was open, says Signe.

I was beginning to wonder if something was wrong, says Signe

and Oline stands there with her one hand resting on her stick and the other holding the pot in front of her, and Oline turns away from Signe and she begins to cross the floor, toward the little room, and her feet are aching and it is horrible that Signe should see what she has done, thinks Oline, because what might Signe think? all of that there? she might just think that all of that has come out of her just now, but in fact only a little bit came out, thinks Oline, and her feet are aching so, but she'll ignore it, they'll just have to ache, as much as they want to, thinks Oline, and she pushes aside the curtain to the little room and she goes to the stool and puts the pot on the stool and so goes out again into the room.

I thought I had to tell you that Sivert is getting worse, says Signe.

You must come now, Sivert asked me to go and get you, says Signe.

Oline nods.

Good if you could come right away, says Signe.

Come with me down the hill, she says

and Oline nods and then sees her drawers hanging down there around her ankles and she goes off and sits down on her chair and she takes a hold of her drawers and pulls them up above her knees, and while one hand is holding her drawers, and the other is on her walking stick, she stands up and hoists her drawers right up.

Yes, you can see how things are, says Oline.

Yes, says Signe.

It's ended up like this, says Oline.

But then you'll be coming right away, says Signe.

Do so, please, she says.

Oline nods.

By the way, there were two half-eaten fish lying outside the door, says Signe.

Fish? says Oline.

Yes, almost eaten up, says Signe.

They were lying just outside your door, she says.

Really? says Oline.

Yes, I must go home again, Sivert is very sick, says Signe.

And I'm coming, says Oline

and Signe did say there were two fish lying outside her door, thinks Oline, what can that mean? surely there hasn't been a cat in her kitchen and stolen her food? no, so crazy, and that Sivert should be lying there dying and wants to speak with her before he dies, and that she, while Sivert is maybe lying there dying, should be sitting up on her table in the room, on her pot, no that will never do, but that's what happened, thinks Oline, and didn't Signe say that the door was standing open? and weren't there two half-eaten fish lying outside? has there been a cat that has stolen her food? and Signe did say that Sivert is waiting for her, so she had better get a grip on herself and go down to see Sivert, talk to him a bit, thinks Oline, she will have to go right away, thinks Oline, and bent over her stick Oline makes her way out into the kitchen, and where has she put those fish? she thinks, she must have put them somewhere, she thinks, and Oline goes over to the kitchen counter and there stands a bowl of water, maybe she put the fish in that, but there aren't any fish there, just a bit of guts and blood in the water, that she can see, but where are the fish in that case? thinks Oline, what has she done with them? thinks Oline, and looks around the kitchen and can't see the fish anywhere, so it must be her fish that are lying half-eaten outside, thinks Oline, and she had better go and see if they are her fish, and she will just have to go down to the sea again to get some new fish, because she must have something to eat, thinks Oline, and if the cat stole her food she had better go and get some more, thinks Oline, she will just have to, and if she is going to visit Sivert all the same, this was almost a blessing in disguise, as they say, thinks Oline and she toddles out of the kitchen, and sure enough, it's aching as usual, but she will ignore it, and she will have to shut the door behind her, thinks Oline, and she toddles over the flagstones in the hall and out of the door, and there just outside the door she can see the half-eaten fish lying there.

Yes, the cat must have been here, she says.

They have to eat too, cats do, she says.

Even cats need food, says Oline.

That's how it is, cats also need food, says Oline

and she thinks that clearly cats need food too, but why not eat up the whole fish? why only half? and why eat two half fish instead of one whole one? thinks Oline, and she shoves first the one then the other fish, toward the wall with her stick.

That's how it is, yes, says Oline

and she thinks that she will have to go down to the sea again, buy herself some new fish, Svein the fisherman will wonder what's going on if she comes twice the same day to buy fish, but that must have happened before, earlier, she must also have gone several times the same day earlier to buy fish again, thinks Oline, sure it's happened sometime, now she'll just have to buy fish again, she thinks, but to be on the safe side shouldn't she have gone to the privy first? what about a little walk to the privy? She should have been to the privy, she thinks, yes she should, she thinks, but she should have taken hold of the fish as well, she thinks, just to be on the safe side, she should have gone, she'll just have to go via the privy, thinks Oline and begins to toddle over to the privy, and sure it's aching, yes, oh dear how it's aching, but there's so much to-ing and fro-ing today that she'll just have to ignore it, nothing for it, she can't just leave off either, not now that the cat has stolen her fish, thinks Oline, and that she can't control herself any longer, that it just comes out as it wants to, that it's got to that stage with her, that it should have done that, no the good Lord will have to release her soon, he let Lars go, and now Sivert is on his way, and soon it'll be her turn, thinks Oline, and she lifts the hook on the door and pushes the door open and enters the privy and sits up on the edge of the toilet, and she sits there, on the edge of the toilet, there sits Oline on the edge of the toilet and pushes the door shut so she puts it on the hook, and next to the hook hangs a picture that Lars once made, a horse, not painted any better than she herself could have done, she thinks, and those brown clouds, she could have managed to paint them herself too, if she had tried, but there is nevertheless something special about that picture, because Lars painted it, that's why there's something special, thinks Oline, no doubt about it, there's something about that picture, and she'll have to get it done again, will have to sit and wait, and get ready again and go down to the sea to get some fish, because she needs something to eat, thinks Oline, and she pulls up her skirts, and she gets halfway up and she pulls down her drawers, and Oline sits over the hole and looks at the horse that Lars once painted and that horse is Lars himself, she thinks, but the horse is her too, that's quite clear, thinks Oline, because both of them can be thought of as horses, thinks Oline, and Lars was quite a scared horse, he used to hide away when people came and knocked on Father's door and Father would open it, and I go into the hall and I see Lars coming out of the room and not looking at me, simply runs past me, his face turned downward he runs past me, and he runs up the stairs and Father looks at me and shakes his head.

He's like that, he says.

He's a cloud, he says.

But that he can't talk a bit with his own sister, that is just too crazy, he says.

I nod and think that sure thing Lars won't talk with me, I knew that he was unwilling to meet people, but that he didn't want to meet me, his own sister, someone he knows so well, no, who can he manage to meet? when he doesn't even dare see me, who can he meet then?

Yes, it's a bit hard, says Father.

But he's not always like that, just now and again, he says.

It even happens that he is eager to talk to people, it's all so up and down with him.

But on some days, no, he doesn't want to see anybody.

And he doesn't say a word to me.

Not a word, and on many days he doesn't say a word to me.

He just sits there, he says.

He varies from being calm and a little shiny-eyed, and then his gaze flickers wildly, says Father.

I can't understand him at all, says Father.

No, I really can't, he says.

I just don't understand him, he says.

No, that's just how he is, I say

and Father says I can come in, and we go into the room and Father and I sit down.

No, Lars is something special, says Father.

That's for sure, he says.

It's not easy to find anyone else like him, he says.

Yes, Lars has always been something special, I say, and Father nods.

And apart from around here he just doesn't want to go any place, he says.

For all the life of him, he doesn't want to go into town.

Doesn't he want to? I say.

Father shakes his head.

No, he's never wanted to all his life, says Father.

No, Lars won't be budged once he's decided on something, then that's how it is, says Father.

But his sister, surely he can manage to talk to his sister, I say.

Yes, I would have thought so, says Father

and I can hear Lars beginning to pace back and forth on the attic above our heads.

Does he pace like that often? I ask in a low voice.

Often, says Father.

Back and forth, I say.

Back and forth, back and forth, says Father.

You know, there's not much floor space to go back and forth on up there, he says.

And he can hardly walk upright, I say.

Yes, that's how it is, in that case, he says.

Yes, yes, he says.

But that's how he is, he says.

He's like that, and nothing to do about it.

People are as they are, he says.

But can I go up to him? I say

and Father says that he has never himself tried to go up to him when Lars is like that, he's never done so, says Father, he's never bothered, because you never know how Lars will take it, he's so unpredictable, says Father, maybe he'll get angry or crazy, he might even enjoy doing so, he says, he maybe doesn't know either, but I can go and try, if I want to, he says.

Yes, maybe, I say.

You can have a try, says Father.

But maybe he won't want to talk with you, says Father.

But you can always try, he says.

Yes, I say

and I get up and Father says that I'm not scared, no, he says and I go with as heavy footsteps as I can muster and clatter up the stairs, I walk as heavily as I can so that Lars will hear that someone is coming up, and I hear the pacing on the attic stop and I see that there is a note pinned up that says Do not disturb on Lars's door and I stop, I can maybe ask Lars whether I can come in, I think, if he wants to talk with his sister, is what I'll have to ask.

Lars, I say

and I'm standing outside Lars's door and I can't hear anything.

Lars don't you want to have a little talk with your sister, with our Oline, I say.

Come on, Lars.

It's me.

Oline, I say.

It's ages since I've seen you, don't you want to talk a bit with me.

It's our Oline, I say.

Come on, Lars, I say

and I can't hear anything from the attic room, and Lars could at least talk a bit with his sister, is what I'm thinking, that he doesn't want to speak to others, with just anybody, that's fine, but he could at least talk with his sister, Lars could at least say a few words to his own sister, I think and I go over and take hold of the door handle and I don't manage to budge the door handle and it moves a little bit, and I grip it harder and the door handle moves a little, gives a little, and there I am holding the door handle, and I press it down a bit, and it gives a bit, so Lars is probably standing pushing up the door handle, I think, that must be how it is, yes, that's how it is, Lars is standing there pushing up the door handle, I think, and how can Lars do such a thing when his sister comes to talk to him, that he doesn't want to talk with his sister, no I just can't understand that, I think.

Lars, you must open up, I say.

It's only your sister, after all.

It's Oline, your sister, I say.

Open up, Lars, I say.

You could surely open up, Lars? I say

and I try again to push down the door handle, but Lars is pushing against me and I can't budge the door handle, even if I use all my strength.

You don't want to talk with me, I say.

Can't you even say a few words to your sister, then, I say.

You can do so, I say

and I try again to press down the door handle, and Lars is pushing against me and I let go of the door handle and I see the door handle fly down and the door fly open, and I can see Lars standing in the doorway holding open the door and everything happens so quickly and I see Lars standing in the doorway and I can see his black hair and beard standing out wildly around his head and his eyes shine black around his skull and Lars shuts the door again and it bangs so loudly that my hands begin to shake and Lars opens the door again and slams the door once more and all around me are loud bangs and the hard black light from his eyes and all I do is stand at the door, right there. And once again Lars opens the door and slams it shut again.

Yes I'm going now, I say.

Can't you see what's written on the door, shouts Lars.

That I don't want to be disturbed, he shouts

and I turn away and begin to go down the stairs and Lars shouts after me that when he's put up a notice that he doesn't want to be disturbed then he doesn't want to be disturbed, I can hear him shouting and I go down the stairs and I hear Lars shouting that people are idiots, they don't understand anything, even his own sister is an idiot, she has no respect for the fact that he wants to do his work, that he needs peace to do his work, I hear him shouting and he opens and slams the door shut again and I go down the stairs and Lars is shouting hell and damnation! women! and those damned painters! shouts Lars and slams the door and opens the door and slams the door and I go into the room to Father and he looks up at me as I come in and he smiles and shakes his head.

He's not quite right in the head, says Father softly.

No, oh no, he's not quite right in the head, he says.

The rage that can seize him.

And the fits of weeping, suddenly he starts weeping, he says.

And just as suddenly he gets angry, starts threatening people.

He's not quite right in the head, Lars isn't, says Father

and I can hear that it's gone quiet up there in the attic.

Now and again something comes over him, I don't know what it is, says Father.

He gets furious, he says.

Or it's weeping.

I don't know which is the worst, I don't, says Father

and I can hear that it is now completely silent up there on the attic, Lars is no longer slamming the door, no longer bawling, no longer pacing the floor back and forth, it's quiet now up there where Lars is. And all I wanted to do was have a little talk

with him, I think. And then he would get as furious as he was just
now, I think, and I hear Father say that I shouldn't get worked up
about Lars, he just is as he is, he doesn't mean anyone any harm,
I hear my Father saying.

Yes, I say.

He just is like that, says Father.

Yes, he just is, I suppose, I say.

Yes, yes, says Father.

I think it's those paintings he paints that make him like that,
says Father.

He's not like an ordinary person, he says.

That fury.

And that weeping, he says.

No, he's not quite as he should be, our Lars isn't, he says.

No he isn't, he says.

But we will have to put up with him, he says.

Yes, I say.

But I think I'll be going now, I say.

That was a short visit, says Father.

I just dropped by, I say

and see Father nodding.

Drop in again soon, then, he says.

I will, I say

and get up, I say bye-bye to Father and ask him to give Lars
my regards and he says he will, we'll just have to put up with
Lars as he is, says Father, the way he is, you have to live your life
as it is, he says, and I nod, and I go out, and Father follows me
out and says we'll see each other soon, that we will, I say, and I
hear Father close the door behind me and I walk and I cannot
quite understand why Lars doesn't want to speak to me, I think
to myself, and I hear trotting steps and I turn around and see Lars
coming running behind me and he is looking down and I stop
and I look at Lars and he is running toward me and Lars stops
in front of me and he is looking down and he says here you are
and hands me a piece of paper with a picture on it and I catch a
glimpse of Lars's eyes and his eyes are moist and he turns around
and begins to trot up toward the house again and I can see on

the piece of paper he has given me, I can see that he has painted on the back of a tobacco box label, and in the picture is a yellow horse and behind the horse are a few bare hills, and a couple of figures that are probably meant to be people, I can see in the picture, standing, as if in mid-air, as I can see, and I can see Lars trotting along up to the house where he and his Father live and I see Lars open the door and go inside. I stand there with the picture that Lars has given me in my hand. I'll begin to walk now, thinks Oline, now she mustn't just sit there in the privy thinking about Lars, that would never do, now that the cat has gone and stolen her fish she can't just stay sitting here, she will just have to summon up strength to get down to the sea to buy herself some fish, she thinks, sitting here is just not on, she thinks, just not on, and when she sits on the toilet nothing comes anyway, thinks Oline, so now she will just have to stop moaning about her aching feet and all the rest and get down to the sea again, it's fine walking downhill after all, she thinks, it's just going back up that's the worst, because the slope is so steep that she only just manages to get back up, thinks Oline and gets to her feet, has to pull up her drawers and now, this evening, she will have to change her underwear, should have done so ages ago, that too, but she must do so this evening, oh yes, thinks Oline and she lifts the door hook and grips her walking stick and how it hurts, how it aches, how it hurts, thinks Oline and she shifts her weight onto her stick, summons up all her strength, moves forward and gets out of the door, does the hook, summons her strength, gets her body moving and so Oline begins to walk down toward the sea, and now she mustn't take any notice of the fact that her feet are aching, mustn't think about it, she'll just have to keep walking and not stop until she gets down to the sea, and there she will no doubt meet Svein the fisherman or one of the others that sell fish, thinks Oline, and she'll go right down to the sea, without stopping, she thinks, no stops, thinks Oline, because when she cannot watch her fish well enough and the cat gets it, then she has not deserved anything but to go down to the sea once again, thinks Oline, and as she has been so daft she hasn't deserved any better, and now, as she passes Svein the fisherman's house, she won't stop, only when she's on her way up the hill, up from the sea, then she'll take a break by Svein the fisherman's house, thinks Oline, so even if her feet ache she will go right down to the sea, thinks Oline, and bent over her stick, she keeps going, as fast as she can, and then Oline hears someone calling, well, are you out and about again, is what is being shouted, and Oline hears that it is Svein the fisherman who is calling.

Yes, you mustn't tell anyone, says Oline

and she stops and sees Svein the fisherman standing outside his house.

Yes, you don't give up, Oline, says Svein the fisherman.

No, no, says Oline.

Are you going into town? says Svein the fisherman.

No, no, says Oline.

Just taking a walk, he says.

Yes, yes, says Oline

and she thinks that now she ought to ask Svein the fisherman whether he's got any fish for her.

I suppose you're on your way to visit your grandchildren, then, says Svein the fisherman.

You wouldn't have some fish for me, would you, says Oline.

So she needs some fish, says Svein the fisherman.

No, I've got rid of the fish I had today, he says.

And you took away a bit of the catch too, he says.

But the cat got the fish, says Oline.

So the cat's been out, says Svein the fisherman.

No, really, he says.

No, that's sad, he says.

But the cat has to eat too, he says.

Sure, the cat's got to eat, he says.

The cat has to live too, he says.

And now you need some new fish, he says.

Yes, that's right I suppose, says Oline

That's silly, says Svein the fisherman.

I've sold my whole catch, he says.

But since it's you, Oline, I'll see if I can't think of something.

I can row out and see if I can't find a little, he says.

I'll row out I will, Oline, and see if I can't find something for you, says Svein the fisherman.

No, that would be too much trouble, says Oline.

No it wouldn't, I understand that I have to help, says Svein the fisherman.

We can go down to the sea together, then we'll see what we can do, he says

and Oline says, no, no, that really is too much trouble, she says, it's horrible of me to trouble him like that, he who's helped her so often with food, says Oline, and Svein the fisherman says that's what we're on this earth for, in order to help one another, he says, and so Oline walks alongside Svein the fisherman down toward the sea, they don't say anything as they walk alongside each other, and Oline thinks that she must ignore the aching in her feet, must just keep on going, like she did in her younger days, thinks Oline, and she hears Svein the fisherman say that they must have food, both cats and people, he says, and Oline says that you have to have food otherwise you can't get by, and Svein the fisherman and Oline walk past the house where Signe and Sivert are living and Oline thinks that she has never been able to get on with Signe, that they have always had something against each other, and in all of her life she has hardly set foot in Signe and Sivert's house, no, that has hardly ever happened, thinks Oline and walking past Signe's house is something she has done so incomprehensibly many times, thinks Oline, every day, during all those years, has she walked past the house where Signe and Sivert are living, and hardly ever has she bumped into Signe, strange that it's been so, they had better avoid one another, those two, thinks Oline, and she hears Svein the fisherman ask how Sivert is getting on, things can't be going so well with him, because hasn't Signe asked twice today for her to come and see Sivert, as he's at death's door, because Sivert is at death's door and wants to talk with Oline, is what Signe said, can't Oline come and talk with Sivert a bit, is what Signe said, that is what she said, that is what she said, wasn't it? it isn't something she's just imagining, thinks Oline, so she will have to go and see Sivert and talk with him a bit, because Sivert is going to pass away and she must go and talk a bit with him, must do, they were the best of friends in her childhood days, her and Sivert, and then he went and shacked up with Signe and she and Signe have never really got on so well, thinks Oline, so she'd better get hold of some fish and then go and see Sivert, and if she's misunderstood, and Signe didn't want her to come, if it's not just something she's imagining, she will have to hide her shame and go to Signe's house, for the first time she can remember, go to Signe's house, no she'd never been in and out of Signe's house, thinks Oline, and she wouldn't have done so today either if Signe herself hadn't asked her to come, and she remembers so badly, she can't remember from twelve till midday as they say, thinks Oline, but Signe did say to her that Sivert really wanted to talk with her, didn't she? and so she will have to go to Signe's because if Sivert is at death's door, and asks her to come and she doesn't come, and she doesn't come, no that would never do, thinks Oline, and she hears Svein the fisherman say that he'll go and row a little way out, and will see if there isn't anything out there for her meal today, nevertheless, says Svein the fisherman and Oline says no, that really is taking too much trouble, she wouldn't have bothered him, wouldn't have asked him for more fish if she had known he didn't have any more, but now she's asked him, now that mistake has been made, says Oline and Svein the fisherman says as long as there are fish, and he gets a bite, that would be fine, says Svein the fisherman, and now her feet are aching so, and maybe something is coming out into her drawers as well? thinks Oline, and if only I could stop for a moment, have a little rest, because she's making such an effort to keep up with Svein the fisherman and he's still good on his feet, even though he must be nearly as old as she is, but he isn't wobbly on his feet, not yet, thinks Oline, and soon they will arrive at the sea, and then she can rest a bit and she can rest a bit, and the aching in her feet will stop, no more is needed, and that'll be good, thinks Oline and she hears Svein the fisherman say that she, Oline, can go and sit down on the bench by the wall of the boathouse, and he will row out a bit, and he knows his fish and it won't take long, he says.

Yes, thank you very much, says Oline.

Yes, we'll have to see what we get, he says.

Yes, you're helping now anyway, says Oline.

Think nothing of it, says Svein the fisherman.

You'd be without food, because I didn't want to row out, he says.

No, you know what.

No, that would never do, says Svein the fisherman

and Oline sees Svein the fisherman go down to the jetty and she herself goes over to the boathouse wall and by the wall is a bench, and Oline sits down on the bench and as soon as she has sat down she feels the aching in her feet ease and she feels how tired she is and now Oline is sitting there by the boathouse wall and can see how Svein the fisherman is untying the rope to the boat and casts off and the boat glides over the sea and Oline sees how Svein starts using his oars and she sees Svein the fisherman row out over the sea, and Svein the fisherman cries out to her that soon he'll have a couple of fish for her, cries Svein the fisherman, and Oline sees Svein the fisherman pull in his oars and take out a piece of line and Svein the fisherman casts the line, and hardly has he cast the line, before Oline sees him get to his feet in the boat and begin to pull in the line with long arms, and Svein the fisherman turns around and cries out to Oline that there he is already, a big one, and Oline sees that he leans over the gunwale and cries out to Oline there he is, a fine cod, cries Svein the fisherman, a really fine cod, he cries, and Oline sees Svein the fisherman lift the cod into the boat.

A fine cod, cries Svein the fisherman.

I'd hardly cast the line but he bit, he says.

A fine fish.

Alive and kicking, very good food, says Svein the fisherman

and Oline sees that Svein the fisherman sits down on the thwart and puts out the oars and so Svein the fisherman begins to row landward and Oline thinks that she will have to go home again with the fish, she can't just sit here, against the boathouse wall with Svein the fisherman's fish, now she will have to toil her way up the hill home again, thinks Oline, and it's going to be horrible toiling her way up the hill home from the sea again, and she will have to toil her way home again, on her aching legs, thinks Oline, and she has no control anymore over what comes out down there, no, it's horrible getting old and if only the good Lord could decide to take her to Himself, that she could be released from all this, that she could now be released from it, thinks Oline and she can see Svein the fisherman mooring the boat and lifting up the fish and come walking up to her with the fish in one hand, no she will have to fasten the fish to the string, she has a string to carry it with, thinks Oline and she sees Svein the fisherman come and stand right in front of her.

Yes, there'll be dinner today too, says Svein the fisherman.

Yes, thanks very much, you really have gone to too much trouble, says Oline.

It's horrible to have to trouble you in this way, she says.

That's all right, it is, says Svein the fisherman.

Have you got some string with you?

Yes, yes, says Oline

and she hands the string to Svein the fisherman and he pushes the string into the one eye of the fish and pushes till it comes out of the other and Oline sees the string coming out through the other eye and Svein the fisherman ties both ends of the string and winds the ends around each other and hands the string with the fish to Oline and Oline presses her walking stick into the soil, and it sinks a little and Oline summons all her strength, now again she will have to summon all her strength, thinks Oline, and now, there, she presses down until she is on her feet and with her free hand accepts the fish that Svein the fisherman is holding out for her.

Yes, thanks very much, says Oline

Thanks a lot.

I'll pay you if only things get sorted out with money, says Oline.

Yes, there's no hurry, says Svein the fisherman.

I'm a bit on the short side right now, says Oline.

I expect so, says Svein the fisherman.

Yes, but thanks anyway, says Oline

and now she must get her body moving, thinks Oline, now she will have to toil her way up the steep hill again, she must get home, she damn well must, yes, as long as she gets home there'll always be a way, thinks Oline, and she hears Svein the fisherman say that he has something he has to do, so he'll be rushing off home, says Svein the fisherman and Oline sees him beginning to walk quickly up the hill between all the houses on the slope, and now she herself is walking up, as long as she gets home, she'll find a way, thinks Oline, she's got to get home, thinks Oline and she gets her body moving and the aching starts up right away, if only she could avoid the ache, may the good Lord release her now, set her free, now she will soon be ready, she too, thinks Oline, and with the fish in her one fist and her stick in the other, Oline pushes her way uphill, step by step she pushes her way uphill and her feet ache so that she can't stand it any longer, it's so bad, thinks Oline, and she'll get home, and she'll go to the privy, and will sit there a bit and see if something comes out, because it's pressing down there, as long as it doesn't come out on its own! as long as she can manage to hold out! thinks Oline, and nothing must come out on its own, no, not now, nothing must come out, not now, as long as she avoids that, thinks Oline, no, not now, she thinks, and maybe is it pressing now? thinks Oline and she is walking bent over her stick, with the fish in her other fist, and Oline lifts her gaze and sees Signe standing there in front of her house, and she doesn't look well, and Oline and Signe have never been the best of friends, no, quite the opposite, no Signe doesn't usually stand there outside her house when Oline is going past, quite the opposite, she would usually rush into the house quick as a flash, when Oline comes along walking, thinks Oline, no she and Signe have never hit it off, and she has never been inside Signe's house, although Signe is married to her brother, to Sivert, and Oline and Sivert were the best of friends in their childhood, little brother Sivert, and he became a handsome man, Sivert did, thinks Oline, but now Signe is standing there and doesn't seem to be going to go inside, she seems to be standing there waiting for her doesn't she, and it doesn't look as if she wants to do anything nice, no Signe doesn't, and Signe is standing there clearly waiting for her, thinks Oline, and why should Signe be standing there like that? Did they not talk to each other earlier today? just think that she can't remember anything about it, she can't remember anything anymore, only a few things that happened a very long time ago, are what she can remember, but those things she can remember clearly and distinctly, that's how it is now, thinks Oline, and the aching, the aching that there is in her feet as soon as she starts setting her body in motion, thinks Oline and she hears Signe say come in now, don't you want to talk with your dying brother, surely you're up to it, says Signe and Oline thinks that her brother is lying there at death's door, that's true, because Signe has said several times today that her brother wants to talk with her, yes, now she can remember, and she goes down to the sea to buy fish while her brother Sivert lies dying, and it really is too crazy how it's ended up like this with her.

You just don't care, says Signe.

You've never cared about anybody but yourself, she says.

But your brother.

It's your brother who's lying there sick and probably at death's door, and can you not be bothered to talk with him a little, she says.

No, can that be right, she says.

It's not right.

It's just too horrible.

And there's not much time left, soon it'll all be over, it might even be too late now.

No, can that be right.

No, it's not right, says Signe

and Oline struggles upwards and stops in front of Signe, she stands there leaning on her stick, with the fish in her other fist.

I've become so forgetful, she says.

I forgot.

I've never had the habit of dropping in on you two, but of course I want to talk with my brother, says Oline.

I should say so, says Signe.

Must come right away, then, says Signe

and Signe begins to walk toward the door and Oline follows and Oline thinks that there's not much left of her, she is so tired, and sure her brother is at death's door, what is she going to say to him? maybe she can ask the Lord Our God to remember her, ask Him for it to be her turn soon, thinks Oline and she goes in through the door into Signe's house and it smells clean in the hall, and everything looks as if it's kept for special days, and there's no lack of anything, thinks Oline, no, she hasn't been in this house often, thinks Oline and she hears Signe say that she will have to come up the stairs, and go to the right through the bedroom, and Sivert is lying in the attic, behind a curtain, says Signe, and stairs are the worst thing Oline knows, getting up the stairs, that's the worst thing she knows, she thinks.

I'll hold your fish for you, if you want, says Signe

and Oline thinks, no, I don't want to let go of the fish, she thinks, and she shakes her head.

But I can surely help you up the stairs, surely I can do that, says Signe

and Oline thinks that she will have to let Signe help her up the stairs, however little she wants her to, but she can do so, because she'll never manage on her own, thinks Oline and Signe grips her walking stick and Signe grips her under her arm and almost drags her up the stairs, and Oline can feel the aches and pains in her feet and Signe is walking one step ahead and she is dragging Oline after her up the stairs and Oline how her feet are aching and Signe drags her up the stairs and gets her to the top.

So, Oline, go in the door to the left, I'll follow later, says Signe.

Have a little talk with him, then I'll come later, says Signe.

I'm going downstairs again, says Signe.

Just call when you are ready, she says.

Or bang on the floor with your stick, says Signe.

That's how Sivert has informed me when he has wanted help, says Signe

and she pushes the stick into Oline's hand, and Oline stands there, with the stick in one hand, with the fish in the other, now she will have to go in to see her little brother Sivert, he's old now, and he's likely to die, is what Signe has said, but he no doubt wants to talk to her before he passes away, is what Signe said, so she had better summon her strength and make her way inside to

Sivert, thinks Oline. She'll just have to, she thinks.

Yes, yes, says Oline.

Yes, yes, she says

and Oline opens the door to the bedroom and she sees a double bed neatly made up, with a crocheted bedspread that covers the whole bed, well that's nice work, thinks Oline, has Signe really crocheted that whole bedspread, well, isn't she hard-working and keeps at it, thinks Oline and sees a large mirror hanging on the one wall, isn't it fine in here, she thinks, and sees a curtain drawn across the middle of the long wall and it'll be behind that that Sivert is lying, in the attic, and she walks across the floor with the fish in her free hand and pushes aside the curtain with her stick, and she goes in and there in bed lies Sivert, gray and unkempt as never before, but on the bedside table lies his pipe, and his tobacco box, and that's a good thing, but his beard is so gray and unkempt and is sticking out in all directions, nobody has clipped his beard for ages, no and his hair is flat and gray, and he has put a hand up under one jaw, long bent fingers, so thin, so thin, stretching up along his jaw, and Oline sees that Sivert is lying there motionless, and next to the bed stands a chair and she'll just have to sit down and see if there's any talk left in Sivert, he has never been a great talker, and he won't be today either no doubt, and his eyes are staring, empty eyes are staring as it seems to Oline and she goes and sits down on the chair and leans her stick against Sivert's bed and holds the fish in her lap.

So, your sister Oline is here, says Oline

and she looks at her brother Sivert, and he doesn't reply.

No, you've never been a great talker, says Oline.

It happened pretty often when you were small that you didn't answer when I said something to you, she says.

You can be sure I remember.

You, Sivert, you, Sivert.

You've always been a bit special, Sivert, says Oline.

Both you and Lars were a bit special, right from when you were tiny tots, says Oline.

But you were never as bad-tempered, you weren't, as Lars.

You, Sivert, you, Sivert, says Oline

and she looks at Sivert's hand that seems to be pressing into his jaw, into the skin.

You can see I've got a fish with me, says Oline

I got this from Bjørn the fisherman.

Well, today the worst thing that could happen happened, Sivert, says Oline.

Today bad things have happened.

I went down to the sea earlier on to fetch a fish, and as usual I got a fish from Bjørn the fisherman.

Two fish was what I got.

And I put the fish down in the kitchen, as usual.

Everything as usual.

But would you believe it, a cat took the fish!

No, how it happened I do not know, but then I saw the fish, the two fish, lying half-eaten outside the house.

My dinner, the cat had run off with my dinner.

That's why I'm a bit late, I had to go down to the sea again to get some new fish, that's why I'm a bit late, says Oline.

But I got a fine fish, says Oline

and she picks up the string with the fish on it and holds the fish up in front of Sivert and he doesn't seem to want to say anything, Sivert, whatever she says or does he just doesn't want to answer her, he must surely be rather hurt that she didn't come, thinks Oline, and Sivert, who asked her to come, so that he could talk with her, because he is old and weary and is at death's door he has asked her to come to talk with him, and now she has come Sivert doesn't want to say a word to her, not one single word does he want to say, thinks Oline and puts the fish back in her lap.

No, you've always been a bit special, you have, Sivert, says Oline.

And I remember you from when you were a little toddler, that I can.

And from when you came to this world, I can remember that.

So stop putting on airs in front of your sister.

And we've always been good friends, you and I, Sivert.

I've seen you grow up, become an adult, get old.

That's what your sister has seen, so now you could say something to her.

You can't just ask her to come and see you and then not say a word when she does get here, no, that just isn't right, says Oline.

No, it's just not right, says Oline.

You really must say something to your sister, says Oline.

You mustn't just lie there, she says

and Oline sees that her brother is lying just the same as when she came in, Sivert is lying with his jaw pressed up against the thin outstretched fingers, his beard is gray and sticking out in all directions, like a bundle of twigs, with his hair on his head, gray and flat, is how Sivert is lying on his pillow and his blue eyes are staring gray and empty in front of him and on the bedside table lie his pipe and the tobacco box, and maybe Sivert wants to have a smoke of his pipe, thinks Oline, he can ask that at least, thinks Oline and she picks up Sivert's pipe and holds it out to him and Oline says that even if he is very sick he could at least smoke a bowlful, she can stop his pipe for him, if he wants, she can light it for him too, even if she is a woman, because she's able to do that, and if the truth be told she would have liked to smoke a pipe herself, if it hadn't have looked so stupid, says Oline and she sits there and holds out the pipe to Sivert, but all he does is lie there, the way he's been lying the whole time, he doesn't even move a finger, just lies there motionless as before, lies there without so much as saying no, does Sivert, thinks Oline, no that he should be so annoyed when she didn't come running right away, no she would never have imagined that, thinks Oline, but that's how he's always been, stubborn and odd, right from childhood Sivert has been stubborn and odd, and once he's decided on something he won't be budged that easily, just like Lars was, both Sivert and Lars were stubborn and odd, they'd never let themselves be budged from something they had decided on, thinks Oline and lays Sivert's pipe back on the bedside table, and both Lars and Sivert smoked a pipe, the two of them both liked pipes, and when they went anywhere they would always take their pipes with them. And they both had long beards, and long hair. First they were black, in both hair and beard, then gray. And Lars had brown eyes, while Sivert had blue ones. But both of them were short and stocky men. And Lars was proud of his beard, when I saw him stroke his beard soft-ly, when he did that several times, I could see he was proud of his beard, I could see the pride in the way he ran his hand through his beard, when he put his pipe in his mouth, above his beard, I could then see that he was pleased with himself, not often mind you, but it did happen that Lars was pleased with himself. And his long hair that he would push behind his ears. And think that that horrible woman cut it off. Cut off both hair and beard. And Lars would hide his face in his hands after that his beard and hair were cut off, no that it should end like that with Lars. I came and visited him when he was at death's door up on the poor loft. And I come in the door and Lars sees me coming and he rolls over in bed and lies with his face toward the wall, and I ask him how he's feeling, I ask him to turn over again, but Lars doesn't want to turn over, and Lars stays facing the wall and brings his hands up to his face, tries to cover his face and tries to cover his scalp where his hair used to hang long and gray and now all that is left is gray tufts and ends. And what have they done with Lars?

Must talk to your sister, I say.

Lars, you've cut off your hair and your beard, I would never have imagined you wanted to do that, I say

and I can hear a thin voice saying that he didn't want to let them cut off his hair and his beard, no not at all, but they did so nevertheless says the thin voice, and I can see that she who is say-ing this is lying curled up in the bed next to Lars's bed, and I can see that she hardly has a face, and I ask her why Lars wasn't al-lowed to keep his hair and his beard, and she says that they said it was because of hygiene, long hair and a long beard needed so much care, and that is why they've cut them off him, and she maybe said that men shouldn't have long hair and a beard, they looked better without, was what she maybe said, is what she may-be said, she says from the bed, but Lars didn't want them to cut his hair and beard, she says, not in any way, she says, and I see Lars lying there, with his face turned to the wall, and he is try-ing to hide his face and scalp with his hands and I hear her say that every time someone comes in he turns away, he doesn't want anyone to see his face anymore she says and she says that Kielland himself, the writer, was here and he wanted to take a picture of Lars, he had a device with him they usually take pictures with, yes goodness me, she says, Kielland himself came to take a photo of Lars, but Lars turned away, toward the wall, and he didn't say a word, even though Kielland himself, the writer, talked to him, but he didn't answer, she says, and after that, she says, Lars didn't let any of the others lying here see his face, and they wouldn't have seen it, they neither, if he could have prevented it, she says and I see Lars lying there trying to hide his face and his scalp.

No, that they wanted to cut off your fine hair and beard, I say.

No, no, that they do something like that, I say.

They do what they want, she says in the bed next to Lars's.

Simply what they want, she says.

And they held him fast, two strong men, and the third one did the cutting, she says.

But it was that wife that wanted him to get rid of his hair, she says

and I can see Lars lying there, turned to the wall, while he is trying to cover his face and his scalp with his hands.

And he never said one word back when Kielland talked to him, she says.

Several times Kielland talked to him, but he never replied, she says.

No Lars, that was stubborn of you, I say.

But I've got a little tobacco for you, I say.

I thought you could need a little tobacco, lying there as you are, I say.

I'll put it on your bedside table, I say

and I go and put the tobacco box on Lars's bedside table and Lars is peeking out at me and I see the heavy black light in his eyes and right away everything seems to be changed, just a glint in his eye, and everything is changed, that's how Lars is too, I think, there's so much going on with that Lars of ours, I think and I say that I'll drop in again and both his hair and his beard are growing back again, so he shouldn't take it so badly anymore, I say and she in the next bed says they come and cut his hair every two weeks and I leave the poor loft and think what is it with people? for all those years the only things Lars was proud of were maybe his big beard and his long hair, and then they go and cut them off both his hair and his beard, what people have become like, I am thinking, how can it have come to this, no, that they can do such things, and it's no doubt the fault of that horrible wife, she doesn't want men to have hair and beards, for her they should have smooth faces and scalps, that's how she wants it, and what's the point if Lars doesn't want them cut, his hair and his beard, all she said was something about that it was God's will that men shouldn't have beards and should have their hair cut short, and if they are nursed by her then they will have to do what she wants them to, or they will just have to look after themselves, and it's because they really can't look after themselves that they end up in the wife's poor loft, I'm thinking and I leave the poor loft and Sivert must soon reply something, thinks Oline, she can't just stay there sitting like that, because Sivert did ask her to come, he wanted to talk with her, is what he said, and now she's sitting by his bed he doesn't answer when she says anything, just like Lars was, he didn't answer either, thinks Oline, and these brothers of hers are like that, they don't answer, but Sivert at least has both his hair and his beard, she thinks, and he must at least answer her.

You asked me to come and see you, says Oline.

Was there anything in particular you wanted to talk to me about, she says.

Well? she says

and Oline looks at Sivert and he is still lying still, with his empty staring eyes, and his fingers pressed into his jaw.

No, then there wasn't, says Oline.

Shall I help you with anything? says Oline.

Do you need anything?

Isn't Signe being nice to you? she says.

Can I do anything for you? she says

and Oline hears footsteps up the stairs and she thinks that this must be Signe on her way.

Signe's on her way, she says.

Your wife, Sivert, she says.

Can you hear them coming? she says

and Oline hears a door being opened and hears footsteps across the floor and that the curtain is pulled aside and Oline sees that Signe has come onto the attic and stands there and looks at Sivert.

You see he's dead, can't you, says Signe

and Oline looks at her brother and he's lying there so peacefully that he could well be dead, she thinks.

Did you manage to talk with him, says Signe.

No, he didn't answer, says Oline.

Yes, in that case you came too late, says Signe.

And just look at you sitting there with a fish on your lap, that's just not right, says Signe.

But now he's dead, says Signe

and Oline can hear from her voice that Signe is about to start crying and she sees the tears running down her cheeks and Signe goes over and closes Sivert's eyelids, and she loosens his hand from his jaw and the skin behind where the fingers were is completely white and Signe turns toward Oline.

You can go now, she says.

You couldn't be bothered to come in time to talk with your brother when he was about to die, she says.

Now you needn't sit here any longer, says Signe

and Oline takes hold of her walking stick and pushes herself to her feet and Oline hears Signe say that she'll help her down the stairs and Oline thinks if she could manage to walk down by herself, that would have been better, but she can't, she can't manage the stairs on her own, no, thinks Oline, and she can feel the ache setting in, and she can hear Signe saying that her chair is all wet, and Oline turns around and sees a puddle on the seat of the chair, no oh no, she is thinking, it's happened again, and she didn't even feel it happen, no, it's got so far with her now, no, now the good Lord will have to have mercy on her too, in the same way as he has taken Sivert away, now it must surely be time for her turn to come, thinks Oline, and she hears Signe saying that it's all going wrong with her, that she can't even hold her water, even when she's sitting at her brother's deathbed, not even then, but she will have to wipe up the piss after her, says Signe, and gripping her arm tightly Signe drags Oline across the floor and Oline just manages to move her feet as fast as Signe wants her to, she can hardly manage to stay on her feet, because Signe is pulling her arm so.

No, you don't care much about your brother, you don't, says Signe.

You could at least have taken the time to exchange a few words with him before he died, he asked me to fetch you.

The last thing Sivert did before he died was to ask me to go and get you.

But did you come?

Yes you did, but too late.

You're a right one, says Signe

and Oline and Signe begin to go downstairs and her feet are aching terribly, thinks Oline, she can feel them aching as never before, and as long as they can get down the stairs and she can leave, thinks Oline, and Signe is nearly dragging her down the stairs and they get down the stairs and Signe lets go of her arm and says that now she'll just have to go off home with her fish, as the fish was no doubt more important than her brother, says Signe, and Oline grips her walking stick in one hand, and holds the string with the fish in her other hand and Oline walks toward the door and she goes outside and she hears Signe saying that the way she didn't care about her brother outdoes everything, says Signe and Oline begins to walk up the hill, she must walk up that steep hill again, because now again, for the second time that day, she has gone down to the sea to fetch fish, and now she will have to go home again and gut the fish, and she will have to ignore the aching, she'll just have to carry on, step by step, and when she reaches the house of Bård the fisherman she'll stop and she'll rest a bit and feel the ache growing less in her feet, and she'll take a break so that her breathing calms down, and she'll go home, she'll go to her little white house, her house that became so nice once she had had it painted white, a white house, with a red door, thinks Oline and she struggles up the hill, and she must get home

with that fish and must then take a rest, because the way she has
trudged with those aching feet, she's had to go twice down to the
sea, twice, simply because a cat went and took her fish and she
found them outside her door, half-eaten, but Bjørn the fisherman
is a good man after all, he helps her, he gives her fish, if it hadn't
have been for Bjørn the fisherman she and her children would
have starved to death long ago, Bjørn the fisherman deserves
many thanks in the Kingdom of Heaven, may the good Lord be
aware of and reward Bjørn the fisherman grandly for all the good
he has done for her and her family, and now she must get home,
and she must go down to see Sivert, because Signe has asked her
to come and see Sivert, he has asked her to come down to their
house, sure he wants to talk with her, Signe said that Sivert had
asked her to come and talk with him, thinks Oline and she creeps
uphill, bent over her walking stick Oline creeps uphill, and it is
aching so in her feet, the ache doesn't seem to want to go away,
even if she only walks a short distance the ache sets in, and the
ache never stops, simply gets worse, and today she has had to walk
twice up the hill, and she will have to go down again once more,
won't she, because Sivert has asked her to drop in and see him
hasn't he? yes, he has, hasn't Sivert asked her to drop in? yes, Sivert
has, thinks Oline, and now she will have to struggle uphill for a
little longer, struggle up the slope, a bit more, thinks Oline, and
when she gets up to the house where Bjørn the fisherman lives,
she'll stop and stand there a while and feel the ache easing, how
her breathing gets easier, how life become livable again, thinks
Oline, and now she will have to push herself, she thinks, just a little bit more, just a little bit more, a little bit more, thinks Oline,
just a little bit more, and she can take a rest, thinks Oline and she
walks up the hill, holding her stick in one hand, the fish in the
other, and Oline is bent double, step by step, and now she will
have to come home to her little beautiful white house, thinks
Oline, now she will have to get home to the house that became so
beautiful, after they had painted it white, with a red door, that
beautiful little house of hers, thinks Oline, and soon she will be
able to stop, rest a little, just a little more, thinks Oline and she
struggles uphill and Oline looks up and she sees the beautiful

white house of hers, but how beautiful, how beautiful it became after it was painted white, yes indeed, thinks Oline and she stops on the hill by Svein the fisherman's house, there stands Oline, with her stick in one hand, the fish in the other, there she stands by her own house and if she stops then the aching in her feet will ease, she thinks, and Oline feels how her feet are aching less and less, how her breathing becomes calmer, how everything inside her gets better is what Oline feels and she thinks that all she has to do is get home, sit down with her knitting, with her crocheting, thinks Oline and now, today, she can even maybe light the stove, because that will be necessary now it has become so cold, and she has firewood, yes she has, she has firewood, but she may have to go to the privy first maybe? have to go to the privy, as long as she gets to the privy before it comes out on its own, as long as it doesn't happen at the back, because she's used to it doing so at the front when there's someone around, thinks Oline, she'll have to live with that, and she really can't stand here any longer, now she will have to walk that last bit home, yes, that is what she must do, she will have to summon all her strength and get her body moving, thinks Oline, and she will have to toil her way uphill for this last bit, thinks Oline, and she puts her stick in front of her and bent double, and with all her might, Oline starts moving uphill, looking down at the ground, step by step she is moving upward and now it is going to come out at the back, now she must hold on till she reaches the privy, get sat down before anything comes out, and she will have to take the fish in the privy with her, she will just have to hang the fish on the hook on the door inside the privy and she won't be able to put down the fish in the house, then it might vanish again, disappear again, thinks Oline and pushes herself uphill and hurries as much as she is able, thinks Oline, but she is going ever so slowly, as long as she is approaching the house, even if she tries to use all her strength to move uphill, and even if she has rested a while and the aching in her feet has eased a while and she's been able to get her breath back. Oline rushes upward and she can see that she is getting near to her house, the beautiful little white house, thinks Oline and now she will just have to go straight to the privy, because nothing

should come out on its own at the back, she will have to get to the
privy in time, thinks Oline and she pushes herself uphill, step by
step, and she can see the red door to her house, but she won't go
inside her house, she'll go to the privy as it is pressing so down
there and she must go right away to the privy, thinks Oline, and
Oline goes around the corner of the house and Oline sees the
privy, and sure it is pressing at the back a hell of a lot, thinks
Oline, and she sees the privy, and she walks as fast as her feet will
carry her, bent over her stick, toward the privy, Oline is moving
and as long as she can make it in time, thinks Oline, and she
walks with the fish dangling on a piece of string, bent over her
stick, and Oline is getting near to the privy and now she will have
to get inside the privy and get sat down, thinks Oline, and she
lifts the hook on the door and Oline gets inside the privy and she
pushes the door shut and no oh no, because something is coming
out at the back, no oh no, something is coming just inside the
door, something has come out thinks Oline and she sits on the
edge of the toilet and sure something is coming out at the back,
thinks Oline, no oh no, that she can't stop herself, and it's getting
worse and worse by the day, that it has come to this with her, and
the good Lord must have mercy on her soon and let her pass
away, thinks Oline, and now she must soon be set free, the Lord
Our God must soon take her home to him, thinks Oline, and she
hangs the fish up on the hook on the door, she's been given a fine,
large fish, and she'll eat it for dinner today, Svein the fisherman
has caught this fish for her, thinks Oline, and Svein the fisherman
has always been good to her, and next to the fish hangs the picture
that Lars painted, a man on a horse, and some hillocks, and everything is painted in yellow and brown and one day Lars came
running after her and gave her this picture, and she never ever
said thanks, thinks Oline, and she never thought the picture was
anything special either, it was more of a daub, is what she thought,
but she accepted it and hung it up in the privy, and there it has
hung for all those years, thinks Oline, and afterwards she saw that
it was a beautiful picture, and she also understands what Lars
meant with that picture, that she does, but saying so! saying what
he meant by it! no, that can't be said, and she finds it impossible

to say, as well, because otherwise there would have been no point
for Lars to paint the picture, then, that's how you can look at it,
thinks Oline, but it's a nice picture, even if it some kind of daub,
the picture is nice, because Lars painted it, a fine picture, that's
what she thinks, yes, if anyone else but Lars had painted it, the
picture is nice, if anyone else but Lars had painted it she wouldn't
have thought it was a beautiful picture, thinks Oline, but she does
think it is a beautiful picture, so beautiful that she nearly gets
tears in her eyes when she looks at it, and she shouldn't do, her old
body, with shit in her drawers, can't get around that, she's sitting
there on the edge of the toilet with shit in her drawers, thinks
Oline and she shakes her head and sees Lars trotting along the
beach and his hair is rising and falling, rising and falling, and I'll
follow him along the beach, thinks Oline, and I can see Lars sit
down on a rock on the beach and he sits there and looks out over
the sea and the wind lifts his hair up, fills his hair, and his beard is
standing out to the side, black hair and black beard in the wind,
and I walk over to Lars and he looks at me and gets to his feet and
begins to trot along the beach, and Lars doesn't want to talk to
me, and he trots along the beach, and he turns around and I can
see those big brown eyes looking at me, and suddenly I see that
his eyes are as big as the heavens, his big brown eyes are as big as
the heavens, and he turns around and cries out to me that I must
leave him in peace and mustn't follow him, cries Lars, and I can
see him getting out of the boat in that fine little velvet suit of his,
and you couldn't recognize Lars, his hair was black and long and
sleek, his hair was, it hung down over his shoulders, Lars's black
hair hung down over his little velvet jacket and under his arm he
has a case made of black leather and Lars smiled to me when he
saw me standing there on the quayside and said that in that case
he had his painting equipment, now I would see what fine pictures he had learnt to paint in Germany, said Lars, now he would
be home this summer and paint the most beautiful pictures, he
said, but in the fall he would go back to Germany, there he would
learn more about how to paint pictures, he had been busy train-
ing to become a landscape painter down there in Germany, said
Lars, and in a couple of weeks I would be able to see what beauti-

ful paintings he could paint, he said, this summer he would be in Norway and paint the most beautiful paintings, said Lars, I would like the painting he was going to paint, said Lars, and so he went off to Mother and Father and to all his other brothers and sisters, and he gave every one of them a good hug, even Father got a hug from Lars that morning on the quayside in Stavanger when Lars came home on summer vacation from Germany, and we went home, and Lars was so handsome walking there in his velvet suit with his black leather equipment case under his arm, with his black hair hanging sleek down over his shoulders. And sure people watched him go by, sure they had heard that he was so good at painting pictures and that the upper crust had sent him to Germany so that he would get better at painting. And Lars walked so proudly along the streets of Stavanger. And then Father said that there had been things about him in the newspaper, they had cut out the articles and there was no end of nice words about him in the newspaper, said Father, and Lars only nodded as he walked along the streets of Stavanger and around him walked Father and Mother and all his brothers and sisters, and I can see Lars's eyes growing wild when Father asks him if he wants to go into town on an errand.

You don't want to, says Father.

Lars shakes his head.

No, then I'll have to do it myself, in that case, says Father.

That's the least you could have done for me, says Father.

But if you don't want to, you don't want to, he says

and I see Lars standing there looking at Father with wild eyes.

I can't really force you, says Father.

But you could at least have helped me, he says.

That really is my honest opinion.

You could at least have done that, he says

and I see Lars standing there and looking down at the floor and I think that Lars never used to be like this before, then he would gladly walk along the streets of Stavanger, but now, now he doesn't want to do so, he doesn't even want to go outside at all, and if he has to go outside he trots along nearby, because for

sure Lars was sent to the asylum in Gaustad to get well again, but
when he came home he didn't want to do anything, I think.

Can't get much help out of you, says Father.

You're a grown man, you could help a little too, he says

and I see Lars starting to run and he runs off and Lars never walks along the streets of Stavanger anymore, Lars never wants
to go into the center of Stavanger, he neither wants to see or meet
people, doesn't even want to meet me I am thinking and I see
Lars running down toward the sea and I can see him sitting leaning against the wall of a house and looking straight up into the
sky, and around his face is a cloud of smoke, and he is sitting
leaning against the wall of a house, and he is puffing at his pipe,
and there is a cloud of smoke around his head, and Lars is peer-
ing straight up into the sky and he sits there grinning to himself
and I then hear him say that he will paint away your picture, he
says, and she mustn't just stay sitting here on the edge of the toilet, inside the privy, she must sit properly, thinks Oline, she can't
just stay sitting like this and not even pull up her skirts, even if a
little has ended up in her drawers, she can't just stay sitting like
this, thinks Oline, and now she will have to manage to sit properly on the toilet, because she can't just sit there looking at the daub
Lars once painted and at that fish of hers that is hanging there,
and shouldn't be hanging here, but should be lying on the kitch-
en counter, gutted and rinsed in fresh water, but now the fish is
hanging there on the door with its big fish eyes! and how they
are staring at her those fish eyes, stiff and black, without light in
them, the fish eyes are staring right into her, that's what it feels
like, thinks Oline, these fish eyes are staring right into her soul,
right in, and even if they do that they don't change their expres-
sion, all they do is stare, they just look and look, they see something, but don't want to reveal what they see, they just see and
see and what can it be that they see? right into her soul? what do
these eyes see inside her soul? do they see something there? can
these fish eyes see something in her soul? is it Lars who is looking
unrecognizably through the fish eyes at her? is it Lars who is looking from somewhere far away through the stiff fish eyes at her? at
her? into her? seeing right into her inner being? if she has any in-

ner being? does she have an inner being? or is an outer being all she has? does she have an inner being? and is it footsteps she can hear, there inside the fish eyes? isn't there someone out there? yes, Oline is sitting looking into the fish eyes and she can hear someone moving about outside, footsteps can be heard and isn't that a voice saying something? isn't it asking if everything is all right and shouldn't Oline then reply that everything is all right, she must say that, yes, that's what she must say, thinks Oline, everything's all right she will have to say, and the voice? was it a man? was it Lars? Lars's voice, was it Lars who was now standing outside her privy, saying something to her? Bård the fisherman? Sivert? And the voice is there again, are you all right, she says, and it's a familiar voice, but whose voice is it? could it be Alida? yes it must have been Alida and Oline hears Alida asking again if everything is all right and Oline thinks that she must answer now and she can't just sit there in the privy and not answer when Alida asks her how she's getting on, then she'll have to answer, thinks Oline and looks into the fish eyes, the black ones, the stiff ones, and the fish eyes look right into her and suddenly she feels she is these fish eyes, she is not the one being looked at by the fish eyes, but she is the fish eyes, Oline realizes and she looks into the black and stiff fish eyes and she is peaceful and the fish eyes are peaceful and inside the stiff fish eyes is something else, something she could never have eaten, however much she had wanted to, and Oline notices that her breathing is peaceful and she really should answer Alida as she talks to her and her breathing is so peaceful, Oline notices and suddenly she feels boundlessly weak and boundlessly peaceful and she sees the fish eyes open up and she sees the light from the fish eyes and from Lars's picture on the wall and never before has she been so peaceful and she slumps against the wall with her head resting against the wall, and Oline feels how a little bit is coming out down there and all there is are the fish eyes and the peaceful light

Norwegian Literature Series

The Norwegian Literature Series was initiated by the Royal Norwegian Consulate Generals of New York and San Francisco, and the Royal Norwegian Embassy in Washington D.C., together with NORLA (Norwegian Literature Abroad). Evolving from the relationship begun in 2006 with the publication of Jon Fosse's *Melancholy*, and continued with Stig Sæterbakken's *Siamese* in 2010, this multi-year collaboration with Dalkey Archive Press will enable the publication of major works of Norwegian Literature in English translation.

Drawing upon Norway's rich literary tradition, which includes such influential figures as Knut Hamsun and Henrik Ibsen, the Norwegian Literature Series will feature major works from the late modernist period to the present day, from revered figures like Tor Ulven to first novelists like Kjersti A. Skomsvold.

Jon Fosse, *Melancholy*

In real life, Lars Hertervig would become, along with Edvard Munch, one of Norway's most renowned painters—but in *Melancholy* he is a promising young artist tortured by doubt and unhinged by unrequited love. After agonizing over his work, drinking alone in a student bar, and obsessively revisiting the loss of his great love, he quits painting entirely, suffers a nervous collapse, and finds himself incarcerated in an insane asylum.

Told with a seamlessly powerful and compulsive voice, the narrator's art becomes, in the end, a means of extricating himself from the tortures of love. "I'll get away from Gaustad Asylum," he says when he's finally released, "and I'll paint your picture away."

Translated by Grethe Kvernes
Scandinavian Literature Series
Dalkey Archive Press

WILLIAM EASTLAKE, *The Bamboo Bed.*
Castle Keep.
Lyric of the Circle Heart.

JEAN ECHENOZ, *Chopin's Move.*

STANLEY ELKIN, *A Bad Man.*
Criers and Kibitzers, Kibitzers and Criers.
The Dick Gibson Show.
The Franchiser.
The Living End.
Mrs. Ted Bliss.

FRANÇOIS EMMANUEL, *Invitation to a Voyage.*

SALVADOR ESPRIU, *Ariadne in the Grotesque Labyrinth.*

LESLIE A. FIEDLER, *Love and Death in the American Novel.*

JUAN FILLOY, *Op Oloop.*

ANDY FITCH, *Pop Poetics.*

GUSTAVE FLAUBERT, *Bouvard and Pécuchet.*

KASS FLEISHER, *Talking out of School.*

JON FOSSE, *Aliss at the Fire.*
Melancholy.

FORD MADOX FORD, *The March of Literature.*

MAX FRISCH, *I'm Not Stiller.*
Man in the Holocene.

CARLOS FUENTES, *Adam in Eden.*
Christopher Unborn.
Distant Relations.
Terra Nostra.
Where the Air Is Clear.

TAKEHIKO FUKUNAGA, *Flowers of Grass.*

WILLIAM GADDIS, JR., *The Recognitions.*

JANICE GALLOWAY, *Foreign Parts.*
The Trick Is to Keep Breathing.

WILLIAM H. GASS, *Cartesian Sonata and Other Novellas.*
The Tunnel. Willie Masters' Lonesome Wife.

GÉRARD GAVARRY, *Hoppla! 1 2 3.*

ETIENNE GILSON, *The Arts of the Beautiful.*
Forms and Substances in the Arts.

C. S. GISCOMBE, *Giscome Road.*
Here.

DOUGLAS GLOVER, *Bad News of the Heart.*

WITOLD GOMBROWICZ, *A Kind of Testament.*

PAULO EMÍLIO SALES GOMES, *P's Three Women.*

GEORGI GOSPODINOV, *Natural Novel.*

JUAN GOYTISOLO, *Count Julian.*
Juan the Landless.
Makbara.
Marks of Identity.

HENRY GREEN, *Back.*
Blindness.
Concluding.
Doting.
Nothing.

JACK GREEN, *Fire the Bastards!*

JIŘÍ GRUŠA, *The Questionnaire.*

MELA HARTWIG, *Am I a Redundant Human Being?*

JOHN HAWKES, *The Passion Artist.*
Whistlejacket.

ELIZABETH HEIGHWAY, ED., *Contemporary Georgian Fiction.*

ALEKSANDAR HEMON, ED., *Best European Fiction.*

AIDAN HIGGINS, *Balcony of Europe.*
Blind Man's Bluff.
Bornholm Night-Ferry.
Flotsam and Jetsam.
Langrishe, Go Down.
Scenes from a Receding Past.

KEIZO HINO, *Isle of Dreams.*

KAZUSHI HOSAKA, *Plainsong.*

ALDOUS HUXLEY, *Antic Hay.*
Crome Yellow.
Point Counter Point.
Those Barren Leaves.
Time Must Have a Stop.

NAOYUKI II, *The Shadow of a Blue Cat.*

GERT JONKE, *Awakening to the Great Sleep War.*
The Distant Sound.

GERT JONKE (cont.), *Geometric Regional Novel.*
Homage to Czerny.
The System of Vienna.
JACQUES JOUET, *Mountain R. Savage.*
Upstaged.
MIEKO KANAI, *The Word Book.*
YORAM KANIUK, *Life on Sandpaper.*
HUGH KENNER, *Flaubert.*
Joyce and Beckett: The Stoic Comedians.
Joyce's Voices.
DANILO KIŠ, *The Attic.*
Garden, Ashes.
The Lute and the Scars.
Psalm 44.
A Tomb for Boris Davidovich.
ANITA KONKKA, *A Fool's Paradise.*
GEORGE KONRÁD, *The City Builder.*
TADEUSZ KONWICKI, *A Minor Apocalypse.*
The Polish Complex.
MENIS KOUMANDAREAS, *Koula.*
ELAINE KRAF, *The Princess of 72nd Street.*
JIM KRUSOE, *Iceland.*
AYSE KULIN, *Farewell: A Mansion in Occupied Istanbul.*
EMILIO LASCANO TEGUI, *On Elegance While Sleeping.*
ERIC LAURRENT, *Do Not Touch.*
VIOLETTE LEDUC, *La Bâtarde.*
EDOUARD LEVÉ, *Autoportrait.*
Suicide.
Works.
MARIO LEVI, *Istanbul Was a Fairy Tale.*
DEBORAH LEVY, *Billy and Girl.*
JOSÉ LEZAMA LIMA, *Paradiso.*
ROSA LIKSOM, *Dark Paradise.*
OSMAN LINS, *Avalovara.*
The Queen of the Prisons of Greece.
ALF MAC LOCHLAINN, *Out of Focus.*
The Corpus in the Library.
RON LOEWINSOHN, *Magnetic Field(s).*
MINA LOY, *Stories and Essays of Mina Loy.*
J.M. MACHADO DE ASSIS, *Stories.*

MELISSA MALOUF, *More Than You Know.*
D. KEITH MANO, *Take Five.*
MICHELINE AHARONIAN MARCOM, *The Mirror in the Well.*
A Brief History of Yes.
BEN MARCUS, *The Age of Wire and String.*
WALLACE MARKFIELD, *Teitlebaum's Window.*
To an Early Grave.
DAVID MARKSON, *Reader's Block.*
Wittgenstein's Mistress.
CAROLE MASO, *AVA.*
LADISLAV MATEJKA & KRYSTYNA POMORSKA, EDS., *Readings in Russian Poetics: Formalist and Structuralist Views.*
HARRY MATHEWS, *Cigarettes.*
The Conversions.
The Human Country: New and Collected Stories.
The Journalist.
My Life in CIA.
Singular Pleasures.
The Sinking of the Odradek.
Stadium.
Tlooth.
JOSEPH MCELROY, *Night Soul and Other Stories.*
DONAL MCLAUGHLIN, *beheading the virgin mary.*
ABDELWAHAB MEDDEB, *Talismano.*
GERHARD MEIER, *Isle of the Dead.*
HERMAN MELVILLE, *The Confidence-Man.*
AMANDA MICHALOPOULOU, *I'd Like.*
STEVEN MILLHAUSER, *The Barnum Museum.*
In the Penny Arcade.
RALPH J. MILLS, JR., *Essays on Poetry.*
MOMUS, *The Book of Jokes.*
CHRISTINE MONTALBETTI, *The Origin of Man.*
Western.
OLIVE MOORE, *Spleen.*

NICHOLAS MOSLEY, *Accident.*
Assassins.
Catastrophe Practice.
Experience and Religion.
A Garden of Trees.
Hopeful Monsters.
Imago Bird.
Impossible Object.
Inventing God.
Judith.
Look at the Dark.
Natalie Natalia.
Serpent.
Time at War.

WARREN MOTTE, *Fables of the Novel:*
French Fiction since 1990.
Fiction Now: The French Novel in the
21st Century.
Oulipo: A Primer of Potential Literature.

GERALD MURNANE, *Barley Patch.*
Inland.

YVES NAVARRE, *Our Share of Time.*
Sweet Tooth.

DOROTHY NELSON, *In Night's City.*
Tar and Feathers.

ESHKOL NEVO, *Homesick.*

WILFRIDO D. NOLLEDO, *But for the*
Lovers.

FLANN O'BRIEN, *At Swim-Two-Birds.*
The Best of Myles.
The Dalkey Archive.
The Hard Life.
The Poor Mouth.
The Third Policeman.

CLAUDE OLLIER, *The Mise-en-Scène.*
Wert and the Life Without End.

GIOVANNI ORELLI, *Walaschek's Dream.*

PATRIK OUŘEDNÍK, *Europeana.*
The Opportune Moment, 1855.

BORIS PAHOR, *Necropolis.*

FERNANDO DEL PASO, *News from*
the Empire.
Palinuro of Mexico.

ROBERT PINGET, *The Inquisitory.*
Mahu or The Material.
Trio.

MANUEL PUIG, *Betrayed by Rita*
Hayworth.
The Buenos Aires Affair.
Heartbreak Tango.

RAYMOND QUENEAU, *The Last Days.*
Odile.
Pierrot Mon Ami.
Saint Glinglin.

ANN QUIN, *Berg.*
Passages.
Three.
Tripticks.

ISHMAEL REED, *The Free-Lance*
Pallbearers.
The Last Days of Louisiana Red.
Ishmael Reed: The Plays.
Juice!
Reckless Eyeballing.
The Terrible Threes.
The Terrible Twos.
Yellow Back Radio Broke-Down.

JASIA REICHARDT, *15 Journeys Warsaw*
to London.

NOËLLE REVAZ, *With the Animals.*

JOÃO UBALDO RIBEIRO, *House of the*
Fortunate Buddhas.

JEAN RICARDOU, *Place Names.*

RAINER MARIA RILKE, *The Notebooks of*
Malte Laurids Brigge.

JULIÁN RÍOS, *The House of Ulysses.*
Larva: A Midsummer Night's Babel.
Poundemonium.
Procession of Shadows.

AUGUSTO ROA BASTOS, *I the Supreme.*

DANIËL ROBBERECHTS, *Arriving in*
Avignon.

JEAN ROLIN, *The Explosion of the Radiator*
Hose.

OLIVIER ROLIN, *Hotel Crystal.*

ALIX CLEO ROUBAUD, *Alix's Journal.*

JACQUES ROUBAUD, *The Form of a City*
Changes Faster, Alas, Than the Human
Heart.
The Great Fire of London.
Hortense in Exile.
Hortense is Abducted.

JACQUES ROUBAUD (cont.), *The Loop.*
Mathematics: The Plurality of Worlds of Lewis.
The Princess Hoppy.
Some Thing Black.
RAYMOND ROUSSEL, *Impressions of Africa.*
VEDRANA RUDAN, *Night.*
STIG SÆTERBAKKEN, *Siamese.*
Self Control.
Through the Night.
LYDIE SALVAYRE, *The Company of Ghosts.*
The Lecture.
The Power of Flies.
LUIS RAFAEL SÁNCHEZ, *Macho Camacho's Beat.*
SEVERO SARDUY, *Cobra & Maitreya.*
NATHALIE SARRAUTE, *Do You Hear Them?*
Martereau.
The Planetarium.
ARNO SCHMIDT, *Collected Novellas.*
Collected Stories.
Nobodaddy's Children.
Two Novels.
ASAF SCHURR, *Motti.*
GAIL SCOTT, *My Paris.*
DAMION SEARLS,
What We Were Doing and Where We Were Going.
JUNE AKERS SEESE, *Is This What Other Women Feel Too?*
What Waiting Really Means.
BERNARD SHARE, *Inish. Transit.*
VIKTOR SHKLOVSKY, *Bowstring.*
Knight's Move.
A Sentimental Journey: Memoirs 1917–1922.
Energy of Delusion: A Book on Plot.
Literature and Cinematography.
Theory of Prose.
Third Factory.
Zoo, or Letters Not about Love.
PIERRE SINIAC, *The Collaborators.*
KJERSTI A. SKOMSVOLD, *The Faster I Walk, the Smaller I am.*

JOSEF ŠKVORECKÝ,
The Engineer of Human Souls.
GILBERT SORRENTINO, *Aberration of Starlight.*
Blue Pastoral.
Crystal Vision.
Imaginative Qualities of Actual Things.
Mulligan Stew.
Pack of Lies.
Red the Fiend.
The Sky Changes.
Something Said.
Splendide-Hôtel.
Steelwork.
Under the Shadow.
W. M. SPACKMAN, *The Complete Fiction.*
ANDRZEJ STASIUK, *Dukla.*
Fado.
GERTRUDE STEIN, *The Making of Americans.*
A Novel of Thank You.
GWEN LI SUI (ED.), *Telltale: 11 Stories.*
LARS SVENDSEN, *A Philosophy of Evil.*
PIOTR SZEWC, *Annihilation.*
GONÇALO M. TAVARES, *Jerusalem.*
Joseph Walser's Machine.
Learning to Pray in the Age of Technique.
LUCIAN DAN TEODOROVICI, *Our Circus Presents...*
NIKANOR TERATOLOGEN, *Assisted Living.*
STEFAN THEMERSON, *Hobson's Island.*
The Mystery of the Sardine.
Tom Harris.
TAEKO TOMIOKA, *Building Waves.*
JOHN TOOMEY, *Sleepwalker.*
JEAN-PHILIPPE TOUSSAINT,
The Bathroom.
Camera.
Monsieur.
Reticence.
Running Away.
Self-Portrait Abroad.
Television.
The Truth about Marie.

FOR A FULL LIST OF PUBLICATIONS, VISIT: www.dalkeyarchive.com

DUMITRU TSEPENEAG, *Hotel Europa.*
The Necessary Marriage.
Pigeon Post.
Vain Art of the Fugue.

ESTHER TUSQUETS, *Stranded.*

DUBRAVKA UGRESIC,
Lend Me Your Character.
Thank You for Not Reading.

TOR ULVEN, *Replacement.*

MATI UNT, *Brecht at Night.*
Diary of a Blood Donor.
Things in the Night.

ÁLVARO URIBE & OLIVIA SEARS, EDS.,
Best of Contemporary Mexican Fiction.

ELOY URROZ, *Friction.*
The Obstacles.

BUKET UZUNER, *I am Istanbul.*

LUISA VALENZUELA, *Dark Desires and
the Others.*
He Who Searches.

PAUL VERHAEGHEN, *Omega Minor.*

AGLAJA VETERANYI, *Why the Child is
Cooking in the Polenta.*

BORIS VIAN, *Heartsnatcher.*

LLORENÇ VILLALONGA, *The Dolls'
Room.*

TOOMAS VINT, *An Unending Landscape.*

IGOR VISHNEVETSKY, *Leningrad.*

ORNELA VORPSI, *The Country Where No
One Ever Dies.*

AUSTRYN WAINHOUSE, *Hedyphagetica.*

CURTIS WHITE, *America's Magic
Mountain.*
The Idea of Home.
Memories of My Father Watching TV.
Requiem.

DIANE WILLIAMS, *Excitability:
Selected Stories.*
Romancer Erector.

DOUGLAS WOOLF, *Wall to Wall.*
Ya! & John-Juan.

JAY WRIGHT, *Polynomials and Pollen.*
The Presentable Art of Reading Absence.

PHILIP WYLIE, *Generation of Vipers.*

MARGUERITE YOUNG, *Angel in
the Forest.*
Miss MacIntosh, My Darling.

REYOUNG, *Unbabbling.*

VLADO ŽABOT, *The Succubus.*

ZORAN ŽIVKOVIĆ , *Hidden Camera.*

LOUIS ZUKOFSKY, *Collected Fiction.*

VITOMIL ZUPAN, *Minuet for Guitar.*

SCOTT ZWIREN, *God Head.*

On the web:

twitter.com/Dalkey_Archive

facebook.com/dalkeyarchive

www.dalkeyarchive.com